THE 101ST SENATOR

THE 101ST SENATOR

CJ HOUY

The 101st Senator
©2023 C.J. Houy. All rights reserved.

Published in the USA by:
CJ Houy
ISBN 978-0-9992187-6-1

Cover Design by JD&J Design
Formatting by Polgarus Studio

ONE

August

Wheeling, West Virginia

A dirty gray pickup exited the interstate and headed onto US 40. It turned onto Bethany Pike and then up into the lush, green hills on the outskirts of Wheeling. Pat Sistrunk followed the route he'd taken so many times. "Oh those hills, beautiful hills," he could almost hear her singing. "How I love the West Virginia hills." He continued humming the tune, not remembering the lyrics to the old state song.

He followed the pike as it wound around the vine-covered trees along the road and climbed up Oglebay Drive into Oglebay Park. As he passed by the lodge, he thought about their honeymoon night. How beautiful she had been and how loving. Then he passed the huge swimming pool, where he'd first seen her—his Edwina, Ed.

He wiped his eyes, wishing she was sitting next to him. She would have been so excited to be here again. Pulling over at the lake, he spied a few couples in paddleboats and recalled their first date. He'd almost fallen in, much to her delight, trying to free their boat from weeds and roots at the shoreline. After reflecting for a few moments, he glanced at his watch, put the truck in gear, and drove into town.

Pat parked at one end of a nearly deserted strip mall in front of Mike

& Ike's Hardware. FOR LEASE signs were posted on several storefront windows and padlocks and chains adorned the doors. Times had been tough for Wheeling for as long as Pat could remember.

In the early 1800s, the National Road first linked the Ohio River to the Potomac and Wheeling became the gateway to the West. In its glory days the bustling city boasted the highest per capita living in the state, but that wealth and popularity had peaked around 1930. The coal and steel town was a shell of its former self.

Ed was born in Wheeling in a house on Edgelawn Avenue that sat behind a long-deserted coal mine. She'd grown up there, and he'd met her at the pool when they were both attending Wheeling College. They were married at St. Michael the Archangel Catholic Church in town before Pat uprooted her for Washington, DC.

The truck door swung open. Summer heat and humidity under hazy sunshine blasted Pat. He eased his corpulent sixty-two-year-old frame out of the driver's seat and stepped onto the pockmarked asphalt. He shrugged a couple times and arched his back. Holding onto the door handle, he stood on one leg and swung his right foot around in a circle. He flexed each knee, then squatted, gripping the handle. Going down was easy, but it was a strain to pull himself up. "Okay, that's enough exercise for today."

Pat stood in front of the hardware store and looked up at its sign. The faded crimson MIKE was overshadowed by a sparkling & IKE. As if Mike had been roasting under a blazing sun for years, while Ike rested in the cool shade of imaginary trees.

A small bell tinkled Pat's arrival in the shop. He moseyed down a tunnel of shelves jam-packed with tools, construction supplies, and lawn care products, as well as pool floats and beach balls for the kiddies, everything covered in nearly an inch of dust. A mustiness permeated the air. Reaching the end of the aisle, he turned and waved at a haggard salt-and-pepper-haired man standing behind the counter.

"Hey, Mike," Pat called.

"Hey, Pat. When d'ya get to town?" Mike's voice held a phlegmy grit with just a touch of Appalachia twang.

"Just now."

"You drive all the way this morning?" The question ended on a downward note, a dialect tic common among the Pennsylvania-Dutch residents of the area.

"Yeah."

Mike glanced at his watch. "Heck, d'ya fly down the highway? It's only ten. It's gotta take . . . what . . . five hours to get here?"

"Yeah, little more, I stopped for coffee, which led to a couple bladder breaks. Heh, heh. Left Alexandria around four a.m." His mouth gaped in a yawn.

"Jeez, that's early."

Pat waved him off. "Yeah, no big deal. I'm not sleeping much these days anyway. Still feels strange in the empty bed."

"I understand. I mean, my bed's always empty, but I can see how if you're used to someone being with you." Mike paused, furrowed his brow, and asked, "You doing okay?"

"Aw, Mike." Pat gave a half wave. "You know, yeah, I'm doing okay. I'm not sure I'll ever get over losing Ed, but work keeps me real busy. I don't get a lotta time to think about it."

"Jeez, Pat. Ike and I are real sorry for you. How long were you married?"

"Forty-two years, right after I graduated. Wheeling College."

"Yeah, ya told me. So, what can I do for you today? How long you staying?"

"I'm here for the August break. I got one more bedroom to finish and then this house'll be done. So I need drywall and paint for an eleven- by twelve-foot room."

"Okay." Mike jotted a note on a small pad. "Color?"

"I think just plain, off-white. Whatever's cheapest, heh, but still decent."

"Who the hell you talking at, Mike?" A wiry, gray-haired African American man bumped his way through the swinging half door from the storeroom.

"Hey, Ike," Pat called as the stooped older man passed behind the counter.

"Well, well, well. Lookie what the cat dragged in. Pat Sistrunk." Ike stood up a little straighter. "Washington bigwig. How you doin' this morning, Senator?" Ike snickered. "Am I s'posed to bow, or kiss your ring?"

"Heh, you're in a good mood. Mike must be treating you right." Pat leaned over the counter and lowered his voice. "But you shouldn't be calling me senator. Somebody might walk in and get the wrong idea." Pat winked at them.

"Yeah, right," Ike scoffed. "And that fool," he motioned toward Mike, "hasn't treated nobody right in fifty years." He turned back to Pat. "You here for another freebie, Pat?"

"Could you do that?" Pat's eyes darted back and forth between Mike and Ike. "I mean, being it's for the church and all?"

"Look, Pat, I'll give you the usual ten percent off," Mike mumbled and shook his head. "That's the best I can do." He stared at the bigwig. "You won't get that from those other guys. But Ike and I try to do our part for the community. Remind me again how this works?"

"Sure, Mike. See, I buy houses that are distressed property real cheap and then I fix 'em up and sell for a pretty good profit. I pay for the supplies and donate my work and give the profits to St. Mike's. This is my fourth house."

"And why here in Wheeling and all for St. Mike's?" the store owner asked as if still a little wary of the out-of-towner.

"Well, that's kinda personal." Pat paused, thinking how to respond. "Well, anyway, just between us, I was kinda lost when I was in college and Father Jerry at St. Mike's helped me out. I'm not sure what would have happened to me without him. And then he introduced me to Ed, my wife, Edwina, at the Oglebay pool. She must've thought I was okay since a priest made the introduction. After that, I swore someday I'd make it up to him. So anyway, that's why."

"That's real generous of you, Pat. I bet the church appreciates it." Mike sounded convinced.

Pat smiled. Resting his hands on the counter, he leaned closer, his eyes dancing, and whispered out of the side of his mouth as if the store merchandise was straining to hear their conversation. "How about twenty percent?"

"Jeez, Pat, I don't know." Mike looked down at the counter.

"Jesus Christ, Mike." Ike glared. "You damn fool. We can't continue to give this guy discounts. How we gonna make any money? What am I s'posed to tell Betty Ann? 'Hey, honey, we gotta eat mac and cheese this whole month'?" He added in a sing-song voice, "'My damn fool partner's giving away the store. Ain't that nice?'"

"C'mon, Ike." Pat smiled. "It's for a good cause."

"Well, I'm a good cause, too, Senator. We aren't all high-paid executives like you Washington dudes. Why you got to pick on me and Mike anyway? We're the little guys. Go cross the river to Belair. Ask Home Depot for a discount. Or that Ace Hardware downtown. We're hanging on by our toenails. What with pandemics, supply chains, price of gas. That shit's killin' us."

"Alright, Ike. That's enough. This is for St. Mike's." Mike's voice was heavier on the grit.

"Wha? You think they named it after you?" Ike shook his head. "You damn fool. You may be my brother, but this brother's gotta eat. We partners, ain't we?"

"Yeah," Mike mumbled, looking down at the scratch pad he'd been writing on.

"Don't forget I saved your life." Ike's voice was rising in volume and pitch.

"Well, don't forget I saved yours!" Mike barked without looking up.

Pat raised both hands, palms out. "Listen, fellows, don't argue. Just make it ten percent." Pat's voice combined a touch of resignation with genuine concern. He smiled. "So, what did you mean about being brothers. You fight together? I heard about guys coming back from Vietnam calling themselves brothers. And saving each other's lives?"

"Nah." Mike put his pencil down. "That ain't it."

"Yeah, we share body parts. If that don't make us brothers, what would?" Ike chimed in.

"What?" Pat's eyes shifted between the two men. He leaned in and whispered, "You guys aren't . . . ?" He cocked his head and leaned away, waving one hand back and forth. "I mean, not that there's anything wrong with that."

"Hell no!" Ike shrieked. "I ought to whup your ass for even thinking that, you sumbitch."

Mike shook his head. "Nothing like that, Pat. Few years ago I was diagnosed with leukemia. Ike, here, gave me bone marrow. Saved my life. Then last year, he needed a kidney and I gave him one of mine."

Mike looked back down at his pad. "So, Pat, I figure the bill will be about five hundred fifty. What say we knock it down by fifty-five bucks?"

"Is that all? I thought you said ten percent?"

Mike looked up from his figures and tilted his head, a curious look on his face. "That *is* ten percent."

"Wow. I figured it'd be more like a hundred. Heh. I never was too good at math. Hold on a second, guys. My phone's buzzing." Pat reached in his pocket and stared at his screen. "Oh my gosh. Listen, Mike. I'm gonna have to take a rain check on the order. My boss is in the hospital. I gotta get back to Washington, pronto."

Ike's eyes followed after Pat as he rushed toward the door. "Well, that explains a lot," he groused.

"What's that?" Mike asked.

"Ain't that damn fool in charge of the government's budget?"

"Yeah, so what?"

"No wonder the country is so mucked up. The guy who's supposed to be balancing the books can't add two plus two and get to four."

TWO

Paris, France

Three in the morning. Heavy rain, mist rising off the Seine. A solitary black-clad figure sits on his idling motorcycle in the middle of the Pont de l'Archevêché. He dismounts and quickly scans his surroundings. All clear.

He flicks open a switchblade knife and jabs it into the seam of the plexiglass siding. With his free hand, he pulls back the barrier. On his knees, he reaches through the opening and grasps the only remaining love lock, the one he hid there four years earlier to keep it safe from the eyes of the bridge authorities. Parisian inspectors had spent weeks snipping off the thousands of love locks that once covered this and other bridges over the Seine. They'd installed the plexiglass siding to deter any future lovers from public displays of *l'amour*.

He wipes the tarnished gold clean, rubs his finger over the etched initials, and secures it back in its hiding spot. He stands up and kicks the plexiglass into place.

He stares down at the black water. The pounding rain bounces off his leather shoulders, saturates his knit cap, and drips from the tip of his nose.

What happened, Melissa? You went to the townhouse on New Year's

Eve when I didn't return? But why were you on the roof? Maybe you were reliving that summer night when we stood on the ledge after the storm and viewed the lights of the city. Then what happened? Something must have gone terribly wrong. Did they push you? He shakes his head no. *They accused me. . . .*

He looks across the river without focusing on the wall of gray buildings on the other side. *I don't believe you would have jumped. That's not the Melissa I knew. She was too smart. Too resilient. Did you fall? That ledge is narrow. And it was snowing that night and you had on those silly sandals with bare toes—in the middle of winter! I saw them in the police photo.* His chest heaves with a great sigh. Once more he shakes his head. *You were clumsy, but in such a lovable, vulnerable way. I remember how you stumbled getting out of my car one night and fell flat on your face. Was that it? You fell? Or did someone push you? Oh, Melissa, I'm so sorry.*

The last time he saw her was at the airport. She was so happy, singing about Santa Claus coming to town, and he was so sad, knowing he had to leave, that he would lose her.

But I never thought that the entire world would lose you.

He sighs again. *I did what I had to do. It was my job. It was essential for my adopted country. They face an existential threat from Iran. But you were never supposed to get hurt. Bad enough what happened to your friend, but you, NO!* his mind screams, *that is inexcusable. I will never forgive myself or Israel for causing you to die, even if it was an accident.*

Her death had been the last straw. He couldn't do it anymore. He couldn't kill for them. *You should know, Melissa, I quit Mossad when I learned that you had died. I will never kill for them again.*

Reaching in his black leather jacket, he pulls out a single red rose, buries his nose in the flower, inhales deeply, then tosses it in the water. "*Adieu, mon amour. Toujours l'amour.*"

He straddles his motorcycle at the exact moment his phone rings, startling him. "Hello?"

"Aaron, I see you've returned," a heavily accented baritone intones.

"Oh, it's you," he snarls. "What do you want?"

"Your country needs you. In fact, the world needs you."

"Pfft. I quit four years ago. I told you." Aaron checks his surroundings but sees no sign of life. "How'd you find me?"

"I knew you'd be back. I know the kind of man you are. Aaron, we need your help. We face a crisis that will make COVID-19 look like child's play."

"Find someone else to do your killing."

"Listen to me. We do not want you to kill anyone. That is, unless, of course, you have no choice," the old man mumbles. "To the contrary, we want you to save mankind. I do not jest. This is no exaggeration." He pauses, as if trying to come up with words to explain. "The world teeters on the brink of a new plague. You must help us stop it."

"I don't have to help you do anything. I don't work for you. Aren't *you* listening?" He clicks off his phone and speeds off the bridge.

From the far side of the river, the gray-haired man lowered his night vision binoculars and turned to his much younger companion, the driver of the black sedan. "We might have our work cut out for us."

He shut down his high-tech optics. "But once he reads the file, he will understand how much we need him. The world cannot survive without him. I am certain his mind will change."

THREE

Maui, Hawaii

"You'll never believe who that was on the phone!" Paula Means-Hayes popped her head into the bathroom and three sets of dark eyes looked up at her.

"Publishers Clearing House saying we won five million dollars?" her husband suggested. He was kneeling next to the bathtub, with his shirt off in anticipation of the splashes from the little boys, and Paula marveled once more at his dark, chiseled physique.

"Ha. I wish, but actually it was something just as shocking and, well, I think almost as fantastic."

Chauncey looked at her and grinned. "Now you've got my interest. How much did we win?"

"No, it wasn't about money, Chaunce. It was Pat Sistrunk. Do you remember him? He's Chairman Lackland's staff director on the Senate Appropriations Committee. Said he was calling me from the road in West Virginia, of all places."

"Wait. Isn't he the guy who fired you? What the fu—," he stopped and glanced down at the two little guys sitting back to back in the bathtub, "heck did he want."

"He wants me to come back. And he didn't fire me. I lost my job when Senator Mitsunaga was defeated. That's what happens to Senate staff. . . . At least, most of the time."

"What do you mean 'come back'? He wants you to go back to DC—to your old job?"

"Yeah! Isn't that great?"

"Great? Are you crazy? Why would you do that? You love your job here. Who'd want to leave Hawaii and go back to that old swamp?"

"Oh, Chauncey. I loved my old job. I mean, sure, teaching democracy to foreign diplomats and military leaders at the Asia Pacific Center is fine . . . it's good. But it's nothing like being the Defense clerk on the committee. There's no better job than that anywhere."

"Maybe so, but DC is no place for me and the boys, it's no place to raise a family, especially one like ours. We fit in here. All we'd get in DC is stares and worse. Plus, the schools aren't great. And what would I do? I don't think there's a call for a Boeing telescope repairman in Washington."

"Mommy, I'm getting cold," Charlie moaned.

"Tell Daddy," she said. She folded her arms, crossed her ankles, and leaned her hips against the doorframe.

Chauncey turned back around and dipped a bright yellow duck-shaped bucket into the warm water and poured some over Charlie's and Ross's curly light brown, almost blond hair.

"I think you guys are done anyway. Stand up and I'll wrap you up, you little sausage biscuits. Your mom's going crazy on us." He pulled the stopper and reached for towels.

"I want Mickey!" Charlie screamed.

"I want Mickey," Ross whined.

"You had Mickey last time, Charlie. It's Ross's turn." Chauncey gave Charlie a faux stern gaze and Paula chuckled.

"But, Daddy, I want Mickey." Charlie tried valiantly to out-whine his brother.

"No buts about it, buddy, you get Donald Duck. Ross gets Mickey tonight. Besides, the Donald Duck towel is yellow. That's your favorite color. You can have Mickey next time."

Chauncey wrapped the two Disney towels around the boys and lifted them out of the tub. "Okay, dry yourselves, put on your pj's, and get in bed. Bring the towels back in here first and hang them up. Your Mom and I are gonna have a little chat." He glanced over his shoulder and arched his eyebrows at Paula.

FOUR

Bethesda, Maryland

"What was so important that it took you all day to get here, Pat?" Beverly Lackland stood next to the elevator in the sterile hospital corridor. It was the VIP wing on the top floor of Walter Reed National Military Medical Center. "It's nearly midnight. Harry's been here since this morning." Her hands were on her hips. She was tapping her foot. Spitting the words.

Pat Sistrunk's shoulders slumped at this reprimand from his boss's forty-eight-year-old wife. "I'm sorry, Mrs. Lackland, but I was in West Virginia when I got word and my truck broke down in the middle of nowhere. After I got it fixed, I came straight here. How is he?"

"Well, thanks to you, he's not doing well. Not well at all. How could you have left him all alone in the Capitol! Are you really that stupid? Luckily, he'd called down for firewood. Firewood!" She threw up her hands. "I mean who makes a fire in August? Anyway, they found him lying on the floor unconscious. Lieutenant Jenson said if the firewood delivery had taken any longer, he would've died."

"Well, thank God someone got there in time."

"They saved his life, but the doctors haven't said how much damage there is. Where were you?" she pried. "You're supposed to take care of

14

him. I can't watch him when he's at work. That's your job."

"I'm sorry, ma'am, I thought you and the chairman were going on a cruise to the Bahamas for the month."

"Oh, no, Harry canceled at the last minute." She waved him off with one hand. "Even with the pandemic all but over, he's still reluctant to get on a boat with three hundred strangers." She scoffed. "Some vacation. But I guess he's got a point. You can't really trust those other passengers. You don't know who they are, their backgrounds." She shuddered. "The last thing we need at his age is for him to get infected by some lowlife. . . . But now this."

Her cavalier attitude about the virus that had taken his wife horrified him, but he resisted the urge to remind her of his loss. Her eyes moistened, and she blinked back the hint of a teardrop. *Wow, that's the first time I've ever seen any emotion from her other than anger.*

Pat thought back to when he'd met her. She must have been about twenty-five. Very cute brunette, with a striking figure and long, thin legs that she liked to display, especially for the senator from Virginia. *I guess it's no surprise he divorced his wife and started up with this one.*

"How did he end up here at Walter Reed, Mrs. Lackland? You said he was at the Capitol when it happened? That's gotta be fifteen miles."

"I insisted they bring him here," she snapped, and raised her nose so high he could see tiny dark hairs in each nostril. "He's a senator. Senators are treated at Walter Reed. It's his right." She punched the air with her index finger. "They wanted to take him to the public hospital at George Washington University." She sounded as if the toney GW was akin to skid row.

"But it's got to take at least thirty or forty minutes longer to get here—even in an ambulance. That's a long time for someone who's suffered a stroke."

Beverly glared. "Are you trying to blame me? Well, listen, bucko. You're dead wrong. They called me as soon as they found him. I was downtown. Unlike you, I got there in minutes. When I arrived, that nice young navy lieutenant from the Capitol Physician's Office, Jim Jenson, was treating him. He and I rode in the ambulance with Harry. I was by his side. You were nowhere around. It's your job to be with him at work. I'm not the bad guy here. You just about killed him." Her brown eyes bore into him.

Pat's shoulders sank a little lower. *Maybe she's right. But how was I supposed to know? Lackland closed the committee. He told the staff to take the entire recess off. Where was his executive assistant? If anyone should have been around in August, it would've been her. And someone must have driven him to work. He hasn't driven a car in at least fifteen years.*

His jumbled thoughts were interrupted by a white-coated middle-aged man approaching them. "Mrs. Lackland?"

"Yes, Doctor? How's my husband?"

"I'm sorry, ma'am, but the news isn't good." The doctor looked at Pat and said, "Would you excuse us, sir?"

"Oh, it's okay, Doctor," Beverly responded. "He works for Harry," she said, jabbing a thumb in Pat's direction.

The doctor nodded to Pat and looked back at Mrs. Lackland.

"Yes, ma'am. I don't know your medical background, so I'm going to put this as simply as I can. Please don't think I'm trying to talk down to you." The doctor forced a weak smile.

Beverly nodded.

"Senator Lackland has had a hemorrhagic stroke. A blood vessel within his brain burst open and leaked blood into the brain tissue. The bleeding kills brain cells almost immediately and damages the brain. By the time he was found, it was too late. He's alive, but we don't see any signs that his cognitive functions will return. I'm sorry."

FIVE

Maui, Hawaii

"You're really sure about this, Paula?" Chauncey threw a penetrating look at his wife. She was seated next to him on the couch on their condo's lanai. The palm trees swayed in the gentle breeze that was removing all traces of humidity from the early evening. Fragrant plumeria blossoms scented the air and the first chirps of the coqui frogs were sounding. The sun had set over Chauncey's left shoulder. The sky was turning into a giant creamsicle. Paradise.

Paula seemed unaware of the idyllic atmosphere. "Oh, Chauncey, we've gone over this a million times in the past two days. I don't know what else I can say." She tilted her head and blinked those gorgeous brown eyes a few times, as if near to tears. She tucked a few stray blonde hairs behind her ear and looked down at her lap.

Chauncey reached over and covered her hand. Her tanned skin was cool and soft.

"Paula, you know I love you. But before we decide what to do, there are some things we need to consider. First, I won't have a job. I can't join Boeing's legislative affairs staff even though I was a liaison in the air force."

"I know. Senator Lackland has a pretty strict policy on conflict of interest. He'd object to the Defense clerk's spouse working for a contractor with ties to the military."

"Exactly. So, what would I do? How could we afford me not working?"

"I've thought about that," she said, turning over her hand and twining her fingers with his. "One, you have your air force pension. That will help us on top of my salary, which is pretty good considering it's a government job. Two, you said you're worried about the schools. The twins aren't even ready for kindergarten yet, but you could stay home and teach them."

Chauncey's eyes widened and eyebrows soared.

"They could even get a head start that way, Chaunce. Heck, you already take better care of them than I do," she said, looking at him imploringly. "This way you could do it full time. And we would save a lot by not having to pay for child care or private schools. And," she paused and showed him that perfect smile that he'd fallen for years ago, "you'd be a great teacher." She let that sink in and then continued.

"I know you like tinkering with things and fine-tuning that multi-billion-dollar telescope on Mount Haleakala. But you've said you're kinda tired of doing the same thing. It's been seven years. This would be something completely new and different and it would be great for the boys."

His mouth twitched but he didn't say anything.

"And, well, you used to like DC. They've got great biking trails, and the restaurants, and it certainly isn't as expensive there as it is here. And wine, Chauncey. Wine! We could get wine from anywhere in the world at reasonable prices. Oh, just think!"

Finally, he unclamped his jaw and said, "Yeah, well, what I think is the boys would never see their mom if you take that job. I know how hard you used to work, and I know how demanding that job is. That's what you were doing when I met you."

Paula released a long breath and looked skyward before training her eyes on him.

"You're right. It's demanding." Her eyes twinkled and she cracked a wide smile. "But we get lots of holidays and we can usually find time to take vacations. How different would that be from now? I mean, you leave before dawn to drive up the mountain for an eight-hour shift. Add on the return trip, and you're gone at least twelve hours. And I'm spending three nights a week in Honolulu teaching. So, I'm not sure the kids would see me any less. Besides they'd have you all to themselves. That's got to more than make up for any lost time with me."

"Damn, Paula. Sometimes I wish you weren't so smart. I never win arguments."

She beamed and lifted his arm around her shoulders. Leaning in close, she whispered in his ear, "But you know I can make it up to you." She took a gentle nip of his earlobe. "You think the boys are asleep yet?"

SIX

September

Washington, DC

"Good morning, Senator Clayborn." Beverly Lackland remained seated on a royal blue couch next to her husband as the recently elected senator from South Carolina strode into Senator Lackland's private office in the Russell Senate Office Building. "Harry told me how pleased he was that you were coming to see him," she said, indicating her husband. "He understands you're seeking funds for a water project outside of Charleston? We just love Charleston. We've had some great times there. Now you just set yourself down and tell the chairman exactly what you're looking for."

Senator Hugh Clayborn stared at the mismatched couple seated on the couch in the dark wood-paneled office, the octogenarian and the middle-aged bombshell.

Mrs. Lackland was wearing a black pants suit with a white blouse open at the collar. A small gold cross hung right below her collarbones. A taut smile stretched across her face while the muscles in her neck seemed to pulse. Senator Lackland, sporting an English tweed sport coat over a powder blue shirt with black slacks, slumped in his seat beside her. His head was tilted to one side and his eyes held a vacant stare.

"Thank you, for seeing me, Mr. Chairman." Clayborn's sonorous voice boomed as he crossed the room. He leaned in and, towering over the old man, offered his hand. Mrs. Lackland snatched it and shook it firmly.

"Now go ahead, Senator," she said. "Set yourself on that chair right there and tell the chairman what you want." Her high-pitched voice held a touch of nervousness and an Arkansas twang. She motioned for Clayborn to sit in the wooden straight-backed chair across from the couch. "We don't have a lot of time. The chairman's very busy. I'm sure you understand. What with the Senate set to return this week and all."

"Um, okay." Clayborn stared at the senator and then shifted his eyes to Mrs. Lackland. Her thin smile had returned. He sat down and leaned forward, resting his elbows on his knees so that he was directly in front of the senator. He flashed a wide grin, showing off his gleaming white teeth. "So, Mr. Chairman, I hope you had a good break. Did you get away?"

"Senator Clayborn, please." Mrs. Lackland interjected. "The chairman has been informed you're looking for ten million dollars to install a new wastewater system northwest of the city of Charleston. Is that correct?"

Clayborn sat a little straighter and shifted in his seat toward the senator's wife. He glanced back at the chairman, who hadn't moved or looked at him. A portly gentleman was standing next to a large window. *I've seen that guy around. He's gotta be Sistrunk, like my staff mentioned.* Clayborn returned his gaze to the dark-haired woman. "Yes, ma'am. That's correct."

Her smile appeared a little less . . . was it threatening or threatened? "Gosh, that's an awful lot of money for one project." She looked like she was forcing herself to smile.

"Well, yes, ma'am, I suppose you could say that," Clayborn

responded. "But it's an area that's growing rapidly and we expect continued growth." He paused and shifted his eyes to the senator. "Those pesky northerners keep invading our southern states." He chuckled. "Virginia, too. Ain't that right, Mr. Chairman?" He reached a long arm out to pat the chairman's knee.

Mrs. Lackland intercepted his attempt, grabbing his wrist. "As I said, the chairman is very busy. Did you bring a detailed project plan, as he requested?" She released Clayborn's wrist and held out her hand.

Clayborn nodded and reached inside his suit coat for a fact sheet. She snatched it, held it up, and waved it back and forth. Sistrunk must have understood the signal. He walked over.

Pat offered him a friendly smile, then took the paper and backed up to his spot next to the window.

Clayborn tracked him with a curious squint. He turned back to face Mrs. Lackland, who was now standing directly in front of the chairman with her hand extended. He stood up and reached out to shake it. With her free hand, she grabbed his elbow and turned him toward the door. "The chairman will review your request. Pat will let your staff know of his decision."

Clayborn tried to look over his shoulder to make eye contact with Chairman Lackland as his wife ushered him toward the door.

"Thanks for coming," she said.

At the entrance, Clayborn turned and leaned close to her and whispered, "Is he alright?"

"Well, of course he is. Now, we'll be in touch. Goodbye." She led him through the doorway and shut the door behind him.

Beverly returned to the couch and collapsed next to her husband. She called over her shoulder, "That's it, Pat. No more meetings."

She felt the fatigue of one who'd just climbed several flights of stairs. She collected her breath. "Harry isn't up to it, you see. You're going to have to handle things from now on." She snorted. "I hope for your sake *you're* up to it."

SEVEN

Yekaterinburg
Sverdlovsk Oblast, Russia

Aaron walked cautiously up three flights of mothball-smelling stairs. He had arrived in Yekaterinburg earlier that day after a lengthy train ride from Paris.

More than a thousand miles east of Moscow, Russia's third-largest city was named after the wife of Peter the Great and was nearing its three-hundredth anniversary. Several sparkling new skyscrapers pushing up the skyline in the bustling city of more than a million surprised him. But this wood building looked as if it had been around since the city's founding. Its walls were speckled with dingy gray paint giving way to patches of bare plaster. Every second or third step creaked. With each sound, Aaron double-checked his surroundings. His right hand was tucked inside the pocket of his black leather jacket clutching a razor-sharp switchblade.

"Welcome, my friend." A middle-aged mostly bald man with hunched shoulders and watery brown eyes spoke softly and smiled. He stood looking down from the top of the stairs. "It's nice to see someone from home." He lowered his voice. "Shalom." Glancing around the empty hallway, he continued to whisper. "Tell me, how are things in Jerusalem?"

Aaron scratched at his month-old beard, burying his fingers in the itchy black steel wool covering his chin. He snorted and shrugged.

"Okay, then. Come inside." The older man closed the door behind them and motioned Aaron to sit at a small wooden table in the rudimentary kitchen. He cleared his throat. "You are no longer Aaron Zimmerman but Mustafa al-Shazir, an Egyptian-by-birth businessman with deep ties to al-Qaeda in the Sinai Peninsula. You're a widower whose wife and daughter were killed in Palestine by Israeli rockets."

How ironic is that? Just reverse the killers with the victims and it's almost my story. Aaron grabbed a chair.

"You have business connections in New York, London, and Rome and trade in diamonds, rubies, and emeralds. You have been brought here to take the virus to the West to release it, which will kill everyone who comes in contact with it." The balding man shuddered and held out a manila envelope.

Aaron peeked inside, spotted an Egyptian passport and several pages of paper. He flipped through them and pulled out a photo of a green-eyed beauty with chestnut hair.

"That is Doctor Borisova. She is an army lieutenant colonel, the project manager of the research team at the Army Artillery Institute. She's a Moscow-trained epidemiologist who was brought here to study coronaviruses. She has been deeply involved in the research. We believe she may have some sympathies for us."

"For Israel?"

"Oh, no. She is virulently anti-Semitic. We believe she sympathizes with the world, knowing the devastation this virus would unleash on all humankind. Well, those of us who are not vaccinated."

"You're saying the COVID vaccines will stop this new plague?" He scoffed. "Then what's the problem?"

"You misunderstand me. The only vaccine that will stop the disease is the new Sputnik hybrid she has manufactured as an antidote. The information you were provided explained that. Their plan is to force the Western world to capitulate to their demands or perish. Only then will they release the cure."

"I see. But why do you need me? If she wants to save mankind, she can give you the vaccine."

The brown-eyed man smiled. "I said she sympathizes with the world. That doesn't mean she is willing to betray her country or her army superiors. And, anyway, what good am I in such things? No, your unique powers of persuasion might be necessary to convince her to provide us the vaccine." His smile turned into a leer as he whispered, "We all know of your success in America. Your charm, looks, and reputation precede you, Casanova. You and your 'Hero of the Republic' medal." He stopped for a moment, then shrugged. "And, if that doesn't work, you will simply have to steal it."

Aaron bristled and stared at the older man. *You son of a bitch. That medal cost me a lot more than it was worth. Why am I doing this? These Mossad bastards are responsible for Melissa's death, even if they didn't push her. Why should I help them again? They probably want me to kill another innocent woman—this doctor.* He closed his eyes and slowly shook his head, recalling the recent phone call and the chilling details in the file left for him. *"We need you to save the world" the old man had said.* He released a heavy sigh. *What choice do I have? She would want me to do this.*

Fracturing the silence, the older man asked, "What else can I tell you?" He folded his arms across his chest. "They are expecting you at the Army Artillery Institute tomorrow morning. There, you'll get more details. They want you to release the virus very soon. But we don't know where and when. We're counting on you, Aaron. Or should I say, Mustafa?" He paused, a very serious look on his face. "The world is counting on you."

EIGHT

The White House

"Mr. President?" Steve Simpson, tall, rail thin, and the president's chief of staff, poked his graying head through the door to the Oval Office. His tone was upbeat, even cheerful, a rarity these days after six difficult years in the same job. "Captain Leroy Jones is here to brief you on our continuity of government plans."

President James Fillmore Parker, the former senator now midway through his second presidential term, sat at the Resolute Desk. He waved them into the room without speaking, then eased his long frame out of the chair and limped around the desk, stopping to flex his left knee and grimacing.

"My old football injury is acting up, Captain, all-conference halfback at UNLV." The president seemed to puff up as he boasted about his former athletic prowess. He took another step, winced, and shook his head. He pointed at the captain's hand. "I see your Naval Academy ring. Football scholarship?"

Steve Simpson glanced at the African American navy captain who was gripping a large roll of papers. The captain jolted upright to his full six feet, but still only came up to the chin of the chief executive. Jones's posture was granite-like. *Oh shit, what a great way to start off the meeting, boss.*

"No, sir, Mr. President. I never played sports," Jones responded curtly. "I was nominated to the academy by Senator Lackland from Virginia."

"Ah-ha. Well, you look like you're big enough. Remind me of that Napoleon Mc-something. You could've . . . oh well, too bad. So what've we got, Steve?" Parker seemed totally unaware of the irritation his football remark had caused. He motioned for them to sit on the cream-colored couch while he slowly sank into an overstuffed gold upholstered chair beside it.

"Yes, sir, Mr. President. Captain Jones is a navy civil engineer, Seabee, in the vernacular. He has the plans for your new underground bunker at Camp David." Steve forced a smile.

"What about the golf course, Simpson? I thought this meeting was about building my golf course," Parker snapped. He edged forward in his chair and turned to look straight at Jones. "Did you know, Captain, there's only one golf hole at Camp David?" He smiled. "Isn't that ridiculous? I'm president of the United States, the most powerful man in the world, and I've only got one lousy hole at my retreat." He slid back in his seat.

"Yes, Mr. President," Steve responded for Jones in a soothing tone. "Now if you'll let the captain proceed." Without waiting for a response, Steve nodded at the navy captain and reached over to unroll the papers lying on the coffee table.

"Okay, uh, Mr. President." Jones pointed at the large satellite image of Camp David and its surroundings on the first page. "You may recognize Camp David in the middle of this picture. As you can see, the camp is surrounded by a fairly dense forest." With his finger, he traced the outline of Catoctin Mountain Park on which Camp David sits. "If we're going to turn this facility into a secure continuity of government site, we'll need to do three things. First, working with the Secret Service, we've determined that the perimeter of the facility needs to be expanded and security bolstered. That will require us to close the popular Hog Neck Trail and the Camp Park Road, which is open to the public from the spring through the fall." He traced two lines on the photo. "Second, the service believes we need to set up a clear-cut buffer zone between the public areas and the camp. This will require us to clear a wide swath of the forest around the camp." With two fingers separated, he drew a circle around the camp.

"That's where the golf course will go, right?" Parker grinned.

Captain Jones winced. "Mr. President, I'm in charge of the continuity of government portion of this project. We're going to build a hardened facility to support the presidency in the event of a national emergency. I don't know anything about a—"

Steve interrupted. "That's right, Mr. President. The buffer zone would be an ideal spot for a golf course."

"We're talking a real golf course, right, Steve? I don't want some rinky-dink par three job. I want a full-up championship-level eighteen-hole course. Lotsa sand traps and water."

"Yes, sir, Mr. President. I'll get to that in a moment if we could let the captain continue." Steve raised his eyebrows, pleading silently with the president to stop talking about the golf course.

"Yeah, yeah. Go ahead, Captain, but be quick about it. I've got things to do." Parker offered a dismissive wave toward the military officer.

Captain Jones flipped to the second page. "And, third, Mr. President, to make this a COG, um, continuity of government site, we would need to build a hardened underground facility with enough space to house fifty individuals, for you and your senior staff. I have the drawings if you'd like me to walk you through them." The captain grabbed the corner of the plans to flip the page.

"No time, Captain, but one question. How are we going to get Congress to pay for this?"

"That's not much of a problem, Mr. President," Steve interjected. "The White House claims executive privilege over its COG programs. We tell the Congress how much money we need, but unless absolutely necessary, we don't give *any* details of what we're doing. . . . To protect the presidency. Article One, Constitution."

"And they go along with that?" Parker didn't sound convinced.

"Generally speaking, yes, sir," Steve replied. "Congress does the same thing. They have their COG plans and we don't question what they're doing. Occasionally, we have to brief the chairmen of the House and Senate Appropriations Committees or their principal staffers. If that were to happen, Captain Jones would make it absolutely clear that the details are on a strict need-to-know basis. Frankly, nobody in Congress needs to know how we protect the presidency. It's too risky. That place leaks like a sieve."

"And we'll use that money to build a golf course?" Parker still seemed unconvinced.

"Not exactly, sir. But if you've heard enough about the secure bunker and plans to close down more of the park, then we can let Captain Jones get back to work. I'll give you the details on the golf course and another issue that demands your attention." Steve motioned for Captain Jones to stand up.

The captain nodded, rolled up his papers, stood, and gave a slight bow toward the president and left the Oval Office.

"Golf course, Steve." President Parker's tone was stern.

"Sir, while we might be able to get away with building a golf course using COG money, we'd probably have a hard time convincing DoD lawyers. But, sir, Camp David is a navy base. We can use navy MWR—morale, welfare, and recreation—funds to pay for the course."

"What's that?"

"All the military departments have recreational activities set up to support the troops, from hotels in Hawaii, Korea, Germany and small beach cottages in various spots, to bowling alleys and golf courses on bases all over the world. The activities collect fees from all these facilities and from base exchanges and clubs, basically, the restaurants and bars. That money is then reinvested in new and existing facilities."

"And Congress goes along?"

"Well, the funds are non-appropriated. That means Congress doesn't provide the money for these things. The customers at the facilities pay user fees," he repeated, "which underwrite the costs of operation. You might have a congressman or two who occasionally get a briefing on MWR, but it's mostly to make sure the troops are getting enough bennies, uh, benefits." He waved his hand dismissively. "So, the kicker here is, we're going to say the golf course will serve as therapy for wounded warriors."

"You're going to lie to Congress?" The former senator squinted at his aide.

"Well, not exactly, sir. We're going to set this up so that wounded military personnel could use the course, too."

"What? I don't want them using my course. They've got their own courses. They must have a half dozen golf courses around here, like the Army Navy Club and the ones at Bolling Air Force Base, or joint base, or whatever they call it. Even the Old Soldiers Home has one, I think. No way, Steve, no way." Parker waved his arms emphatically.

"Mr. President, if I may." Steve paused, hoping the bluster would subside. "First, the only way we can get them to build you a golf course is by making it a navy activity. Second, it would only be open to wounded warriors. *And*," he thumped his index finger on the coffee table, "*only* when you're not there. So, Mr. President, you'd never see or hear other golfers."

"But I don't want them on my course." Parker crossed his arms and sneered.

"Mr. President, how many wounded war veterans are going to make a trip up to Camp David to play golf? I mean, how many who live in this area can even play golf? We're talking paraplegics, sir. There can't be very many. This is how we get you an eighteen-hole championship-level golf course. It's the perfect solution." Steve stared at the president.

Parker glared back at him.

"And, Mr. President, one other subject, if I may."

"Make it quick, Steve." Parker flipped on the TV.

"Sir, the Israelis have informed the DNI, that is, the Director of National Intelligence, that the Russians are working on a new and deadly COVID strain."

"They're wrong." The chief executive pointed the remote control at the TV and changed channels to the golf channel. "If it's COVID, it's Chinese, Steve. That's why everyone calls it the China virus. The Chinese are the ones who do COVID. Besides we've got vaccines now. What do we care?"

"Yes, sir. But the Israelis say—"

"And why would we believe them? They stole our space laser."

"Well, maybe. The head of Mossad told the CIA director that a Senate staffer *gave* them the plans for the laser. They didn't steal it."

"A likely story. Do they think we just fell off the turnip truck? Anyway, COVID is Chinese."

"Yes, sir, I understand your hesitancy to believe it. But our intelligence community is saying with a high degree of certainty that the Israeli claim looks legitimate."

"Yeah, well, these so-called experts don't know anything anyway. Allen Dulles and Bill Donovan would roll over in their graves if they knew what these fools were up to. We need some real men in intelligence. Old-fashioned spies, cloak-and-dagger stuff. Now it's all drones and satellites and freaking weather balloons. These guys couldn't find an enemy spy if he was in the same room."

"Well, Russia is apparently working—"

"Russia, Russia, Russia. That's all they think about over there. I know Putin. He wouldn't do that." He stopped talking and raised his index finger. "The next guy who comes in here and says Russia is doing something like this, I'm firing his ass." He glowered. "And that includes you, Mr. Smarty-Pants." He lowered his finger and pretended to fire it in Steve's direction.

NINE

Dirksen Senate Office Building

"Defense Appropriations, this is Paula." Paula answered the phone that sat on her hundred-year-old mahogany partners desk. She leaned back in her chair in her new office on the first floor of the Dirksen office building.

"Paula?"

Paula snapped to attention, immediately recognizing the deep, melodious voice of her former boss. *Wow, talk about déjà vu.*

"Senator Mitsunaga, what a surprise. How are you, sir?"

"Oh, fine, fine. I heard through the grapevine that you were back at the committee. I thought you and Chauncey were enjoying yourselves making babies here in Hawaii?"

Paula could feel herself blushing. "Um, gee, senator, um . . ."

He chuckled. "But I'm not really surprised you'd go back. That life can suck you in, even with the long hours and canceled vacations and things." He paused for a moment but didn't give her a chance to respond. "Your Chauncey's a good man. I hope you didn't have to twist his arm."

"Well, maybe a little. But, yes, sir, he's the best. It just took me a while to figure that out."

"After my campaign and all that went on, I'm not surprised you finally settled down, Paula. An experience like that can leave a bad taste in your mouth."

"Yes, sir, losing was a huge disappointment for me. I can only imagine what it felt like for you."

"Oh, it wasn't so bad. I didn't imagine I would win with all the garbage that preceded it—Chinese spies and, well, betrayal. I only wish they'd have let me rely more on you for the campaign."

"Gee, Senator, that's nice of you to say. But I didn't know the first thing about running a campaign like that. I mean, I still don't, not really."

"I think I would have been better off, considering the results."

"Well, yes, sir, thanks again. I learned a lot on that campaign. You might find it strange, but for one, it did make me realize what a great guy Chauncey is. So, even with all the, um, disappointment, it worked out well for me. I just wish the same was true for you." *Why's he calling? I know him well enough. He doesn't call to chat.*

"So, how's your new chairman—or does she call herself 'chairwoman'?—the gal from California, Liz Boyer? Sam Jackson, you know, my old friend and partner, calls her a lioness." He ended with a chuckle.

"Well, sir. I've been pleasantly surprised, or maybe a little relieved. Before I took the job I asked Jeff Leary about her. I replaced him. Do you remember Jeff?" she asked.

A muffled "Mm-hmm" from the senator.

"Jeff was on the legislative subcommittee staff when you were here, sir." Paula racked her brain trying to make sense of this conversation. "Anyway, he told me she'd mellowed—that's the word he used—since her early run-ins with Senator Jackson. But unfortunately Jeff's little girl is very sick with something called neurofibromatosis. His health insurance won't cover the costs, so he had to quit to go make more money. Pat Sistrunk offered me the job. He said that Chairman Boyer insisted he hire a woman, and he thought of me." She stopped for a quick breath.

"But you're right. Chauncey and I love Hawaii," she continued to ramble. "We'll be coming back one day. We even kept our condo on Maui. But, Senator, you know how I loved this job—and working for you." She quickly added the last bit, as any good staffer would, to assuage the ego of the former legislator. "When Pat called, Chauncey and I talked it out, and honestly, I guess I dragged him and the boys here, but so far he's doing okay playing Mr. Mom." She squirmed in her seat.

"So how are you? Is there something I can do for you?"

"As a matter of fact, yes, I'd like to ask a favor. I believe it's very important."

"Yes, sir, I'll do anything for you. I hope you know that." *Okay. Maybe we're finally getting to the point.*

"Well, thank you, Paula, it means a great deal. In that case, I'd like you to meet with an old friend of mine. He has some information he thinks people in Washington need to hear. But he's come up against a brick wall in trying to share it."

"Okay, sir," Paula said, puzzled over this ask. "But in case you don't know, we aren't doing earmarks in Defense anymore, if this is about a Hawaii project."

"No, no. This isn't about Hawaii. My colleague didn't go into detail, but he says the matter is very grave. His name is Ari Schweitzman. I've known him since my days on the Intelligence Committee."

Intelligence? Ari? "Um, gee, sir, he wouldn't be Israeli, would he?"

"Oh, yes. How did you guess? Now, I don't believe he's any sort of intelligence officer, but he does have very close ties to the government in Jerusalem. Over the years he's shared a great deal of sensitive information with me."

Crap. What do I do now? I can't meet with the Israelis, not after that debacle with the space weapon and the deaths of those staffers. "Sir, I'm not sure what to say. Israel isn't exactly in good graces these days. It's not like when you were here. I'm sure you've heard the rumors about them stealing our weapons and maybe worse?"

"I'm well aware of that, Paula. But I trust Ari and no one in our government will listen to him. I suggest you meet with him and hear him out. Then you can decide whether the topic should be pursued."

"Gee, sir. You know I'm required to report my meetings with foreigners. I'd have to document it if I meet with him."

"I understand. But, Paula, sometimes you have to bend the rules."

She opened her mouth, but stayed quiet.

"As I said," the senator continued, "meet with him. Listen to his story and then decide how to report it. You could tell your chairman, or Sistrunk—you mentioned he's still working for Harry." He stopped speaking. She could hear his finger tapping. "Perhaps you could wait to report it to the authorities until you have to renew your security clearance. That wouldn't be so bad, would it?"

Paula rolled her eyes and stifled a chuckle.

"Paula, I wouldn't ask if I didn't think it was crucial."

"Yes, sir. But why me?"

"Ari knows all about you. And since I trust you, so does he. And, Paula, he said this matter is very, very grave."

Her shoulders slumped. "Okay, sir. I guess I can meet with him, but I have to report it to someone afterward."

"Very good," Mitsunaga sounded satisfied. "He suggested you meet this evening at six thirty at Blue Duck Tavern. He's scheduled to leave for Jerusalem at midnight. Will that work for you?"

Tonight? Foggy Bottom. Crap, crap, crap. Chauncey's gonna kill me. "Um, yeah, I guess so, Senator."

"Very well, then. And, Paula?"

"Yes, sir?"

"Thank you for doing this. And thank you for taking my call. I know you don't have to do that any longer, and I want you to know I appreciate it."

"Gee, Senator. Of course I took your call. I'd do anything for you, sir." She ended the call. *But this? Oh boy!*

TEN

The Capitol

Gracie Shelten, a middle-aged, medium-height bottle blonde in a Kelly green dress a little too tight for her pudgy frame, leaned her head in the open door of the staff director's cavernous office. The office boasted gold leaf trim, a working fireplace, and unobstructed views of the National Mall, the Washington Monument, and the Lincoln Memorial in the distance. "Pat, Mrs. Lackland's on the main number. She sounds a little irritated."

Pat Sistrunk leaned back in his chair and emptied his lungs in one long release. He sat up, smiled at his assistant, and said, "Thanks, Gracie." He muttered to himself as she departed, "Okay. Here we go. I gotta tell her." He punched the button for the main line and lifted the phone's receiver. "Hi, Beverly. Thanks for calling me back. We got an issue that can't wait."

"Well, what is it? And it's 'Mrs. Lackland' to you. I'm not some young bobble-headed staff assistant you can chase around your office."

"Yes, ma'am. Sorry. Listen, we've only got a couple weeks till the end of the fiscal year. Our appropriations bills won't all be finished by then. We're gonna need to do a CR—that's a continuing resolution— so government won't have to shut down on October 1."

"I know what a CR is!" she shot back.

"Okay, and—"

"Well, just do it."

"Yes, ma'am. But it's not that simple."

"Well, it's your job to make it simple, bucko. You wanted this job, remember. You were his driver, then you snookered him into making you a professional staffer on the committee and weaseled your way up to become staff director. Now those chickens are coming home to roost, aren't they? Do your job. It's just a CR. Harry can't be bothered."

Pat shook his head slowly and closed his eyes. "But, ma'am, it means holding a full-committee markup." He lowered his voice and whispered, "How's the chairman going to hold a markup? He can't even hold his head up."

"Don't you disparage him, you jerk! Have a little sympathy. Maybe he can't manage a markup *right now*. You'll have to find someone else to do it."

"But how are we going to explain that? It's bad enough he missed two votes last week. Luckily, the leader isn't doing much on the Senate floor. But soon, the press is going to be all over the chairman's story. There's already chatter spreading that something is wrong." Pat shifted in his leather chair and took a deep breath. "You can't hide this forever. Seriously, Bever—, um, Mrs. Lackland, shouldn't you be talking to the leader about having the senator step down? I mean, I love the guy, but he isn't all there. It's not right."

"I'll tell you what's not right, you stupid fool! It's your management. Harry is going to be fine. I just know it. We have to be patient. Give him a little more time. Find some excuse and have someone else chair."

He heard the phone receiver slam down.

ELEVEN

The Capitol

Longtime newspaper reporter Harris Ward of *Roll Call* leaned against the wall in the Brumidi Corridors of the Capitol. He looked up from scrolling through news stories on his phone as Pat Sistrunk exited the Appropriations full committee suite of offices. Harris adjusted his tortoiseshell glasses and brushed his gray-brown hair off his forehead. He took three giant steps over to Pat. "Hey, Pat, got a minute?"

Pat turned to face him. It was clear Pat recognized him before glancing around, as if checking who else might be listening in the dimly lit hallway, its walls and ceiling covered in the spectacular nineteenth-century murals painted by Constantino Brumidi. "Hey, Harris. How you been? Haven't seen you around much. Your CNN gig keeping you from wandering the halls?" He chuckled. "And on that subject, how come you're on TV? I thought you worked for *Roll Call.*"

Harris offered a thin smile and nodded. "Yeah, I'm trying to do both. Not sure it's worth it, though. I'm getting a little old for this. Know what I mean?" He smiled and paused. *This guy's acting like he's not busy, but they're marking up the CR next week.* "How's the CR coming? You need to do it next week so it's finished before October, right?"

"That's right, just like every year." Pat chuckled again.

"You look like you haven't got a care in the world," Harris lied.

Pat did another quick survey of the area and spoke in a hushed tone. "Let me share a secret, on deep background." He grinned.

Harris cocked his head. *What's his game?* Pat Sistrunk wasn't the kind to leak sensitive information. He wouldn't still have a job if he was. "Sure, what's up?"

Pat whispered, "The secret is I hire smart people." He bobbed his head almost like one of those dolls with the spring in its neck. "They do all the work." He snickered. "So, Amber, my deputy, is putting the bill together with Floyd Carruthers. She's sharp as a tack and Floyd's got thirty years' experience writing CRs. I'm going down to the carryout and grab a sandwich while they work out the details. Have a good day, Harris." He slid by Harris headed in the direction of the elevator.

"That's great, Pat. Real clever." Harris followed right behind him. "Say, I haven't seen the chairman around for a week or two. With the CR coming up, I wonder if I might get a few minutes to talk to him. Can you help me out?"

Pat stopped and slowly turned around. He stood there for a second too long, as if trying to figure out the right thing to say. "Gee, Harris. Can't help you with that. He's too busy working on the CR. This isn't a good time." He turned and pressed the elevator button.

"But I thought you said it was . . ." Harris paused and looked down at his pocket-sized reporter's notebook, "Amber and Floyd who did all the work? Why would they need to bother the chairman? I mean, if they're so smart?" Harris kept his face a blank canvas to avoid smirking.

Pat's smile morphed into a frown as he turned back around. "Can't help you, Harris." He took a short breath and erased the frown. "Tell you what." He leaned forward, squinted, and wrinkled his nose like a mouse checking out a piece of cheese. "Chairman Lackland likes you. I'll talk to him and see if he could spare a few minutes. I'll let you know." He got on the elevator.

That was weird. *Sounds like a bunch of BS. Chairman Lackland hasn't been seen for weeks. He missed last week's votes. And now he's unavailable for comment. All very fishy. I'll ask around. Somebody must know what's up.* Harris wrote himself a note and slipped his notebook inside his sport coat.

TWELVE

Foggy Bottom, Washington, DC

It was still light outside on a pleasantly cool late-September evening when Paula popped out of the Foggy Bottom metro station. She headed north several blocks to the Blue Duck Tavern in the Park Hyatt hotel. The tree-lined streets were jam-packed with cars vying to exit the city and the sidewalks were filled with well-dressed men and women all rushing for the metro station, presumably on their way home.

Paula arrived at the hotel and scanned the seating area on the patio. The email she'd received indicated Ari would be waiting there. She spotted a very old man in a dark suit sitting in a wicker chair at a bleached wood table reading a newspaper. He had found a spot away from the other patrons in a corner next to a short ivy-covered brick wall with a row of thick conifers behind him. *That's got to be him.* She walked over and offered her beautiful smile. "Excuse me, Mr. Schweitzman?"

He looked up from his newspaper with watery blue-gray eyes. A few meandering gray strands on his head fluttered in the gentle breeze. He nodded and cleared his throat. "Yes, Paula." His voice was a deep baritone. He started to stand and motioned for her to sit. "Thank you for agreeing to meet with me. I am sure you are very busy with the fiscal year coming to an end."

The prominent blue veins on his thin, age-spotted hands caught her attention. She relaxed a little at the sight of this grandfatherly figure and sat catty-corner from him.

"Can I get you something to drink?" He smiled, presenting a calm visage. With a twinkle, he added, "I understand you like red wine."

Paula flinched. She took a deep breath as her smile returned. "No, thank you. I have to drive home," she lied.

Ari gazed at her curiously, as if he knew she took the metro. "Very well. Shall I get right down to it?"

A tall, dark-haired waiter approached, menus tucked under one arm. "Good evening, ma'am. Can I get you something from the bar to start?"

Paula looked up and shook her head. "No, thank you. Just a glass of water. I can't stay." She offered that smile with the sparkling white teeth, the one that had won her runner-up in the Miss Virginia contest nearly two decades earlier.

"Of course, ma'am. And you, sir, another cocktail? I have a menu if you're planning on dinner." He pulled the menus from beneath his arm.

The old man waved his hand still staring at Paula. "No, sir. If my beautiful young friend cannot keep me company, I shan't dine alone."

Paula watched the waiter depart and said, "So, Senator Mitsunaga said you had some very important information to share. First, may I ask, why me?"

Ari folded his hands on the table and leaned in. "I guess the simple answer is because my old friend Ken Mitsunaga trusts you."

Paula tilted her head back and raised her eyebrows, saying nothing.

"Now a more complete answer." He paused and whistled under his breath. "Where to begin?" The old man nodded a few times and pursed his lips. "You, of course, know that the good senator was the chairman of the Intelligence Committee many years ago. I had the opportunity to discuss with him matters of great security importance to the Israeli government. We got to know and trust one another. He was a strong supporter of Israel and Jewish people worldwide." He smiled. "In Israel they say there are more trees planted in Senator Mitsunaga's honor than for any other noncitizen of my country. Sadly, he has left the Senate or, I can assure you, I would be sharing my concerns with him now." He paused and scanned the patio for a moment before refocusing on Paula.

"I am an old man. My friends in Congress have mostly retired or passed. The doors to Congress, which were once wide open to me, are shuttered." He frowned. "Your government officials no longer trust me. But this matter is of such dire importance that I must persist. Paula, you are my last hope." His deep voice had taken on a more urgent tone.

"Why should *I* trust you? Israel betrayed us with the space laser." She glared at her companion.

"No, my dear, that is incorrect. What you are referring to was a most unfortunate incident. But I can assure you, Israel stole nothing. The plans for that weapon were given to my country."

"But Israel killed that Senate staffer."

"That, too, is false. We did nothing of the sort. Now, can I assure you that a rogue agent, acting on his own, I must emphasize, might have done something like that? No, I can't. He has denied it to our authorities. And I have no reason to doubt him. I can say unequivocally the government of Israel was not the cause of that young woman's unfortunate death." He stared at her with a look that begged to be believed.

Paula said nothing.

"But that is ancient history. The US and Israel must set aside our disputes. The crisis coming is too grave to let such bygones get in the way." He balled his hands into fists. "The Russians have manufactured a virus for which the only antidote, a vaccine, is in their hands. They plan to force the world to capitulate to their policy goals or they will kill us all. Can you imagine? We might have to relinquish the West Bank. You, disband NATO. Who knows exactly what they will demand. But we will be helpless to stop them." He pounded his fists on the table and glanced at the other patrons when the cutlery rattled.

Paula also looked around. No one seemed to notice. She leaned forward and said in a low voice, "If what you say is accurate, why isn't our intelligence community up in arms?"

He shook his head and threw up his hands. "It is unbelievable. But what we are being told, as hard to fathom as it is, is that the White House insists no one is to raise questions about Russia and viruses. They have convinced themselves only the Chinese would do such a thing."

"That's crazy." She leaned back in her seat. "I don't believe it."

He leaned across the table. "Yes, it is crazy. But is not your chief executive just a little crazy?" He gave a half smile as he sat back.

"Yeah, well. But how do you know this? I'm sure the Russians aren't broadcasting this on the news."

"We have a source inside the army institute where the Russians continue to explore biological agents. Our evidence is ironclad. We have seen the impact in an experiment their scientists conducted. This new disease is designed to look like a coronavirus, but it is far worse than COVID. It will kill anyone who comes in contact within days. It is as deadly as anthrax and more contagious than COVID's Omicron or Delta. In short, once released, there will be no containing it. Unless we are successful in replicating the vaccine."

"So, why tell us? Even allies keep secrets."

"We need your help—"

"My help!" she exclaimed. "What can I do?"

"Israel doesn't have the ability to reverse engineer the antidote. We believe only your infectious disease people at Fort Detrick in Maryland have the skills necessary to carry out such a task. They have decades of experience dealing with biological agents, no?"

"I don't run Fort Detrick. Besides, if the White House is denying this even exists, how could the army help? They have to follow orders."

"I know it is a stretch. But what else can I do?"

Her mouth fell open and she threw up her hands.

His watery blue-gray eyes locked onto hers, but his voice was placating. "I am an old man. My time is due. What would it really matter if I caught the plague? But you, you are young. You have children to protect." He stared at her for a moment and scratched the back of his head. "I am out of ideas. The only thing I can do is send up the warning. Senator Mitsunaga said you work miracles. So, I am here seeking divine intervention. Please help. Ask questions. Tell your superiors. But, please, please help. You are our last hope."

THIRTEEN

Yekaterinburg

Aaron Zimmermann, now Mustafa al-Shazir, slowly zig-zagged his Lada Riva sedan through the faded red-and-white-striped Jersey barriers and approached the rusty vine-covered gate. He craned his neck. No guards anywhere. "This doesn't look right," he muttered.

A decrepit telephone hung on a wooden pole to his left. He reached out the window and picked up the receiver, not expecting to hear anything. He did a quick check of his image in the rearview mirror. His dark beard was thick and bushy beneath his dark eyes and sallow visage.

"What is your business?" A scratchy voice came through the receiver speaking Russian.

Startled by the request, he stammered, "Um, this is Mustafa al-Shazir. I am expected." His Russian was not great, but he managed to get the words out, as he had been instructed.

A buzzer sounded and the gate groaned open. He passed through and followed the road, swerving around potholes and an occasional sapling sprouting through the crumbling paving. He drove up to a nondescript rectangular three-story 1950s Soviet-style concrete building. Its only flourish was a hammer and sickle relief in faded red and gold paint above the entrance. He parked and surveyed the area, counting nearly a dozen cars. Most looked rusted out and abandoned. Only a couple looked drivable.

Three concrete steps led to an entryway. The door was locked. He pressed a grimy yellow intercom button on the wall and the same scratchy voice demanded, "What is your business?"

He repeated his message in Russian and heard the door click open. He nudged it with his foot and stepped inside, checking his surroundings in the dingy gray-walled corridor. To his right, down a center hallway, he spotted an open door leading to a well-lit room. He approached and knocked on the metal door frame.

A shapely chestnut-haired woman in a white lab coat hunched over a counter. She glanced around without moving. Then she stood up straight and turned to face him while removing her black square-rimmed glasses. She had to be about five ten, nearly eye level with him, and she approached with an outstretched hand. Her smile was thin but friendly, no teeth. She used her free hand to pull the white coat closed over her ample chest. The pungent fragrance of lilac filled his senses as she neared.

"Dr. Borisova?" he asked.

She nodded. "And you are?" she asked in Russian.

"Mustafa al-Shazir. Do you might speak English? My Russian weak."

One corner of her smile widened. "Yes, of course. How do I call you? Mr. Shazir, or is al-Shazir more proper?"

"Mustafa would be fine." He returned the smile and shook her hand.

"Natasha."

He chuckled. "Your parents had a sense of humor."

"*Shto*?" She cocked her head.

Oops. Of course they didn't have Rocky and Bullwinkle *reruns in the old Soviet Union.* "Unimportant." He threw up a dismissive wave and looked around the room. "Why do we meet here? This place looks abandoned."

"Yes," she inhaled deeply, "unfortunate because collapse of Soviet Union. But good cover from eyes of NATO, others."

"But how can you conduct research in this place?" He swept his hand around the nearly empty room.

"Not for you worry," she snapped. "Your job deliver product. No?"

"Yes, of course. So, tell me the plan. Where am I going and who will I infect?"

She frowned. "In time will know details." She crossed her arms. Her eyes scanned him with a look that seemed to ask, *Can I trust this man?* "So, I understand you travel America and West Europe. Correct?"

"Yes, my business sends me to all the Western capitals. But I want to be clear from the beginning: I am not seeking eternal salvation and the one hundred virgins that come with martyrdom." He cracked a smile. There was no reaction from the doctor. He tried again. "Look, I'm not a suicide bomber. How will I survive if I spread this new . . . disease?" He dropped the smile.

"I give antidote. You give self after infect targets. Vaccine very powerful. Even if sick from virus, once inoculate self, you fine."

"And I am to trust you that all this will work?"

"As I must trust you not compromise mission."

FOURTEEN

Dirksen Senate Office Building

A thirty-something brown-haired man of medium height and build stood in the doorway to Paula's office. His fist was readied to rap on the doorjamb. Dressed in a Brooks Brothers suit, with gleaming oxfords, he might have just stepped out of the store's catalog.

"C'mon in, Stevie," Paula said from her seat on the couch. Stevie Guy nodded and entered. He looked around at the new artwork on the walls. Gone were the sailing pictures on loan from the Smithsonian. Framed paintings of warships and airplanes, on loan from the Pentagon, now covered the walls.

"You better shut the door. Or you think we need to go to the vault to discuss this?"

"No, ma'am." He popped the top of a spring-loaded stop and the heavy door swung shut. "The agency isn't saying much, but the briefer really squirmed in her seat when I brought it up. Sounds like your information might be close to the truth."

"I was afraid of that. And it's 'Paula,' not 'ma'am.'" She smiled. "I mean, if Senator Mitsunaga thought it was so important that I meet with this guy, it seems likely his concern would be warranted." She sighed. "God help us. Any thoughts on what I should do, Stevie?"

"Boy, that's a tough call. What can we do about this kind of thing? We're just staff. Maybe you should tell the chairman and see what she thinks." He paused for a second and shook his head slowly. "But, from what I've seen, Boyer's not fond of surprises, or Israel." He lowered his voice. "And with what happened on the space laser program, she's not alone."

"Yeah. Probably not the best way for me to get to know her better is to say my former boss told me to meet with an Israeli. I tell you, Stevie, everything about that guy screams Mossad. Even if Mitsunaga says he isn't a spy. I feel like I should've had the security spooks scan me for bugs after I sat with him for ten minutes. It was kinda creepy."

Larraine Walker, the admin assistant, knocked and then popped her coiffed gray head through the doorway. "Paula, Pat Sistrunk's on the main number for you."

"Okay, thanks, Larraine." She walked over to her desk and picked up the phone. "This is Paula."

She listened as Pat spoke.

"Sure, Pat." She hung up and said loud enough for the other two to hear. "Gotta go to the Capitol. He sounded funny, maybe irritated or nervous or something. Wonder why he didn't use the intercom?"

Larraine, listening at the doorway, chuckled. "He said he couldn't remember your number."

"Hey," Stevie chirped. "Why don't you tell Pat about that Israeli meeting? That way you can claim that you've reported the contact to your superior. That is, in case the FBI starts tapping around."

"Good thinking, Stevie. Senator Mitsunaga suggested the same thing." Paula's brown eyes sparkled and that perfect smile lit up the room. "Maybe that'll keep me out of jail."

FIFTEEN

The Capitol

Paula felt a little déjà vu entering S-128, the anteroom of the Appropriations Committee's suite of offices. She stared up at the vaulted ceiling. The large gold shield and emblems of war and peace formed an ornate framework above the windows on the western end of the expansive room. This room, one of six designed by Constantino Brumidi, was originally for the Military Affairs Committee. Revolutionary War battle scenes wrapped around the tops of the walls. She was enthralled by its incredible beauty each time she entered.

She sighed as she passed through the staff offices, glancing at the desk right outside of Pat's door that had briefly been hers. She knocked once on his door frame and walked in. It was her first visit since she'd returned to the committee.

The staff director was leaning back in his ergonomic black leather desk chair. His feet rested on the desktop, his striped tie askew. The buttons on his white dress shirt strained to stay fastened. She glanced over at the open doorway to the chairman's small private office adjacent to the staff director's huge space. The lights in the chairman's office were turned off.

Okay. At least the big boss isn't here. Deep breath.

"Hey, Pat. You wanted to see me?"

"Grab a seat, Paula." He motioned for her to take one of two straight-back mahogany chairs with black leather seats in front of his massive desk.

Paula sat down, sitting rigidly, both feet on the floor, knees together. A legal pad was tucked under her arm, which she repositioned to her lap to cover her bare knees. She twirled a pencil with three fingers of her right hand as if it were a majorette's baton.

"What's up?" She tried to maintain a calm demeanor even though her stomach was one big knot.

"Heh, heh. This might sound a little funny, but I need your help."

Paula forced a smile. "Sure, Pat. What can I do for you?"

"So, uh, Paula. We need to mark up the CR in committee next week. We've got to make a couple changes to the House-passed version. Technical stuff really, but the minority is insisting on a formal markup. And the leader wants the CR on the floor on Thursday. So Tuesday is the only day we can hold markup."

Pat interlaced his fingers and cracked his knuckles before continuing. "But the chairman, well, he's not able to be here. He's got a family matter to attend to in southern Virginia." He blinked a couple times. "It's a private thing. Well, anyway, he'd like Senator Boyer to chair the meeting."

"Really? Boyer? But she's one of the more junior members. Why her?"

Pat stood up and walked around the desk and tried to perch himself on the corner, but he was too short. Using both hands, he attempted to lift himself onto the desk. Paula had to suppress a giggle as he hoisted himself up, his large belly bouncing with each effort. He gave up after a couple of tries.

"Heh, heh," he laughed. "Guess I'm not as young as I used to be." He leaned against the desk instead. "So, anyways, like I was saying. Lackland wants Boyer to chair." He leaned a little closer to Paula and lowered his voice. "You see, Senator Lackland really trusts Liz Boyer. You know, if it weren't for him, she wouldn't be chairing the Defense Subcommittee. Boyer owes him. He knows it. She knows it." He leaned back and swiped his hands together like he was dusting them off. "So he's confident she'll chair, with no funny stuff." He threw a stern look at Paula that quickly changed into a grin. "Besides, she's tough. She won't put up with any guff if the minority guys try anything. And, you know," he shook his head slowly, "you can never be sure what the other side'll try. It's not like the old days, when you were here before with Mitsunaga and Sam Jackson, where most everyone got along. Nowadays we're more likely to fight over the stupidest stuff than to just take care of business." He shook his head again. "Lackland hates that. But it's a sign of the times. Long story short, Lackland trusts Boyer to get this done. Understood?"

Paula nodded.

"Good. Now I need you to tell her."

"Me? Why me? Don't you think the chairman should ask her? Wouldn't it be better if he just called her?"

"Nah, he doesn't want to do that. You tell her. Heh, heh. That's why you get paid the big bucks."

Paula looked down and sighed.

"What's the problem, Paula? She'll probably welcome the chance to run the show. Get her name in the paper. Besides, you guys are pretty much done. If anyone asks, I'll say he chose her because her Defense bill is already in conference. And, anyway, it's your agreement with the House that has forced us to re-divvy up bucks. Redo the subcommittee allocations. That's why the minority is insisting on a formal markup. Besides, most of the other subcommittees are crashing. They're still putting their bills together or waiting to go to the floor."

"Yeah, okay, Pat. I guess you're right. It's just . . . I'm still getting my feet on the ground with her. I can tell she doesn't trust me yet. She doesn't really know me. I mean, you've been with Lackland for, what, twenty years?"

Pat nodded. "More than that."

"And I worked for Mitsunaga for a decade. It takes time for them to trust us. We got to earn our stripes. Right now, I'm still the new guy, well, gal. It's no secret she wanted someone else as her clerk. You put me there—and, once again, thanks for that—but I'll have to work hard to get on her good side, get her to believe that I've got her best interest at heart. If I'm the one to pass on this message, she's bound to wonder whose interest I'm serving." Paula looked at Pat with raised eyebrows.

"Nah, Paula." He flapped his hand dismissively. "You're making a mountain out of this mouse hill. She'll be fine." He leaned in again and lowered his voice. "And you know she won't want to tell the chairman no." He pulled back and puffed himself up. "Nobody, tells Lackland no. He's the chairman. Now go tell her." He raised his hands palm side up, as if excusing her.

Paula stood up and turned to leave. *Yeah, right. If it were that easy, why wouldn't you call her yourself? Something's fishy about this.*

"Okay, Pat," she said over her shoulder. "I'll call her. Tell her Lackland's indisposed."

"Indisposed? Why'd you say that? He's not indisposed." Pat's voice rose with each word until he was almost shouting. He cocked his head and squinted. "Did somebody say something about him being indisposed?" He snapped, "If they did, they're wrong. He's not indisposed. It's a *fam-i-ly comm-it-ment.*" He emphasized each syllable.

Paula felt her eyes bug out a little and she leaned away from the bombast. "Jeepers, Pat. No, I didn't mean anything by that. It's just an expression. I'm sorry if I gave you the wrong idea. Nobody said anything. He's okay, isn't he? The chairman, I mean."

The muscles in Pat's face relaxed a little, but he jerked straight up with her question. "Of course he's fine. He, uh, can't be here on Tuesday. And, if Boyer says anything, tell her the chairman won't take no for an answer."

Paula nodded and walked away. Halfway to the door she spun around. "Oh, Pat. There is one thing I need to mention." She walked back over. Pat had plopped down in his chair, and she stood in front of his desk. "So, Mitsunaga called me and asked me to meet an old Israeli friend of his." She leaned over the desk and whispered, "I think he could be Mossad, you know, an Israeli spy, but Mitsunaga swears he isn't." She straightened up. "Well, this Israeli told me his government thinks the Russians are manufacturing a deadly virus that they'll use to blackmail us and maybe the Israelis or Europe and Japan. He says the White House is ignoring the intel and has buried its head in the sand. Because Israel is PNG."

Pat looked up with an apparent lack of understanding.

"PNG, Pat. *Persona non grata*, it's Latin. It means someone we won't talk to. Like when we kick diplomats out of the country for being spies. And, well, after that thing when the Israelis stole that laser weapon, even though this guy denied it, well, anyway Mitsunaga says no one will listen to this Israeli. But, man, if he's right, this is terrible. And I don't know what to do."

Pat's expression still hadn't changed. "Why are you telling me?"

"Well, I guess, first, because you're my supervisor, so I'm reporting the contact I had with a foreigner. Second, because I thought maybe you'd have some idea of what we could do about it. And, third—"

"Sounds more like something you guys on Defense should handle. I've got a CR to worry about. You need to take care of this yourself. Now, if you'll excuse me, I got a call to make." He waved her away.

Paula stepped into the corridor outside the Appropriations Capitol suite and spotted *Roll Call* reporter Harris Ward lingering in the hallway. "My, my, Harris Ward. How are you? It's been a long time."

"Hello, Paula. I heard you were back. How did they drag you out of Hawaii?" He returned her smile.

"Hah. You should know better than anyone. This place can capture you. I mean, you've been covering the Hill longer than anybody. Weren't you here when LBJ was leader?" Her eyes twinkled above her grin.

"Yeah, right. More like Howard Baker, twenty plus years after Johnson. But I know what you mean. Once you're here it's hard to quit. It's addictive."

She nodded. "I think it's like a merry-go-round. While you're here, you're spinning around at a blistering speed, the music is blaring, and you're bouncing up and down. Sometimes you think it's making you too dizzy; it's too loud; you got to get off. But when you do, the merry-go-round keeps spinning, and you watch it, and you start to miss the bouncing up and down. And, before you know it, the folks spinning around have forgotten your name and you wonder why you got off this ride. Anyway, all that means is I had a chance to get back in the game and jumped in." She paused, glancing back over her shoulder at the doorway she just walked through. "But you know I'm already starting to get dizzy. Not sure things make sense these days."

Harris frowned and nodded.

She shook her head. "Anyway, so why you lurking in the hallway?"

"Pat promised me a meeting with Lackland. But I can't seem to get on his calendar. Did you talk to him? I didn't see him come in this morning."

"I talked to Pat. If you mean Senator Lackland, no, he wasn't in."

"Not surprised. Haven't seen him in days. Rumors starting to swirl that something's wrong. He's at that age when any unforeseen absence starts a death watch. Sad to say."

Paula grimaced. "Beats me. All Pat said was he won't be here for the CR markup. A family commitment. Weird, huh? But if he promised you an interview, it must be a coincidence."

"Well, in my business we don't put much stock in coincidence."

SIXTEEN

Yekaterinburg

Mustafa al-Shazir's apartment building was on the southern outskirts of Yekaterinburg, about twenty kilometers from the artillery institute. Aaron sat on a corner of the thin mattress in the tiny third-floor studio staring out the filthy window at the gray Russian day. Through the grime, he could see a forest at the edge of town.

The ancient radiator was hissing and spitting but creating very little heat. At last a little filtered sunshine broke through the clouds, enough to provide some warmth.

The mission was not going well. The meeting place at the artillery institute clearly was not where the vaccine and virus were manufactured. The intelligence he had was woefully inadequate, and his escape plan was too risky.

Borisova obviously doesn't trust me. Perhaps it's time to catch the train out of here. But if I fail, the world faces a catastrophe. Somehow I must gain her trust and get the vaccine.

But how? What could he offer to break down the barriers?

She is a beautiful woman. Maybe my contact is right. Maybe I can charm her.

He stood up and approached the window. The clouds closed

overhead, blotting out the sun. Except for the glimpse of dark green forest in the distance, the entire world seemed monochrome. More gray than sepia, dingy, dirty, dank. And, though it was only September, freezing cold as if it might snow any moment.

He slipped on a thick gray wool sweater and grabbed his leather jacket. He glanced around the room. All was in place. Pencil shavings lay on a scrap of paper on the floor near the door. If anyone entered while he was gone, he would know. He carefully pulled the door closed behind him and locked it.

SEVENTEEN

The Capitol

"Where's Harry?"

Pat Sistrunk bolted to attention at his desk as the majority leader's voice snarled over his cell phone. "He's not in the office today. I believe he's at home, sir. Do you need him?"

"What the hell's going on? Is he okay? Nobody's seen him since August. He missed the last three votes. All I'm getting out of Beverly is that he's working from home. Aren't you marking up the CR tomorrow?" Charley Johnson, the senior senator from South Dakota and longtime Democratic leader, was clearly irritated. But his terse language was typical. It almost seemed like he hated talking on the phone. An anomaly among politicians. They generally reveled at the sound of their own voice, welcoming any chance to drone on and on.

"Yes, um, si . . . sir." Pat stumbled over the words. He always struggled with how to address the majority leader. Should he call him Mr. Majority Leader, or Leader, or Senator Johnson? He settled on sir. Most members realized the terms *ma'am* and *sir* connoted appropriate respect. *But don't use that term with Senator Fox. She feels that calling her ma'am instead of Senator shows a lack of respect. She snaps the head off of any staffer who dares call her ma'am.*

Pat's hand trembled as he held the phone. Lying to a person as powerful as the leader was not good policy, but he had to protect his chairman.

"So he'll be here tomorrow when you mark up? You tell him I want to talk to him when you see him."

"But—" The line went dead. Pat stared at his phone. *Okay. I didn't lie. We are marking up tomorrow. He didn't give me a chance to tell him the chairman won't be here.*

Pat figured he'd tell Chairman Lackland that the leader wanted to talk to him the next time he saw him. It just wouldn't be tomorrow.

EIGHTEEN

Dirksen Senate Office Building

"Okay, gang, what do we know?" Paula tucked a loose strand of blonde hair behind her ear and glanced around her office at each of her staff members. "Mindy, O&M?"

Broad-shouldered, pudgy, and with sandy hair, Mindy sat up a little straighter. "Nothing new in Operation and Maintenance, boss. Sitting on our hands. The House is holding up the conference report until we file the new 302b, the subcommittee allocations. The Speaker apparently doesn't trust us to keep our deal. He wants proof that the Senate will support the new allocations and our conference agreement before he lets the House vote. Besides that, the army's whining, the air force is fuming, the marines saluted and said, 'thank you, ma'am, whip me again,' and the navy's not saying nothing." Mindy paused to take a swig from her beer. "That's actually got me a little worried," she mumbled.

"Why's that?" Paula perked up.

"If they're not pissed, I musta done something wrong. It's like they got a billion stashed away somewhere that we didn't find. And, once the bill's signed into law, they'll come clean. Or maybe they won't say nothing, but they'll be chortling over there across the river."

"Okay. Got it. What about you, Stevie? Anything I need to know?"

Stevie Guy looked up from his seat on the other side of the room. "Nah, like Mindy said, we're all waiting for this dog to die. Hopefully, it'll be soon. Like fish and visitors, Appropriations bills start to smell after a few days. At least the conference report was filed with the House Rules Committee, so all people can do is complain. They can't change anything." Stevie opened a red file folder on his lap, making sure its contents could not be seen by the other staffers. "On another subject, not in the bill, but I got a tip on a COG thing that's a little curious. If you got a moment after we're done?"

Paula gave him a quizzical look. "You referring to continuity of government?"

"Yes, sorry. Shoulda said that," Stevie apologized.

"Senate's or president's?" Paula asked.

"His. I'm not cleared for ours." He chuckled. "If we even have one."

"Ditto," Paula said. "I'm sure Congress has some plan. But it must be the full committee's problem. Not squirreled away in our bill. As far as I know," she mumbled the last part. Paula scanned the room. "Anybody else got something I need to know about? I'm going to see Chairman Boyer and I want to apprise her of any issues out there."

She looked at each one in turn. No one spoke up. She smiled and let out a relieved sigh and slapped her hands on the couch cushions. "Good. Thanks, everyone. You guys did great work. I know Jeff was pleased with the job you all did before he retired. Now I'll get the credit for it." She laughed. "But don't think I don't know and appreciate it. And, I promise, I'll make sure people know it was you all and Jeff who deserve the praise. Or the blame, Mindy." She winked at the pudgy woman, who was sitting with her feet up on Paula's desk.

Mindy guffawed and tossed her empty beer can in the recycle bin.

NINETEEN

Yekaterinburg

Inside Dr. Borisova's spartan office, an opaque glass door pushed open. From where he was sitting, through the opening, Aaron spotted a staircase leading down. One corner of his mouth curled up with a hint of a smile. *Aha. A basement. That must be where the lab is.* A stooped gray-haired woman with deeply wrinkled ashen skin stopped bustling in when she saw his sallow, bearded face. Her brows lowered and she glared.

Dr. Borisova turned and barked something in Russian that Aaron didn't understand. She waved the woman in and pointed to a wastebasket. The little old lady turned away from Aaron, muttering something, and shuffled across the room. She emptied the trash into a tin five-gallon bucket, turned, and limped back through the doorway.

"Jew." Borisova spat out the word.

"What?" Aaron instinctively reached inside his jacket pocket for his switchblade.

"That old woman. She is Jewess. Only good for one thing. Empty trash. And I wish she not do."

"In my country, I'd shoot her." He sneered.

"Sadly, law no permit. But I insist they have only menial task."

Aaron forced his features to remain neutral. "So, I saw the staircase through the door. Is your laboratory downstairs?"

"Yes, I guess good time to show. Follow me."

She opened the door and proceeded down the stairs. Aaron followed, noticing how difficult it would be to get in and out of the lab with this being the only entrance. Borisova reached in her pocket and pulled out a key to unlock the door at the bottom of the staircase. Inside was a long hallway with glass-walled rooms on each side. Aaron quickly counted seven lab employees. Each wore full hazmat gear.

"I see everyone is in protective clothing. Are we safe?"

"I am. I have vaccine. You should be okay. Don't open doors." She chuckled.

To his left behind a thick glass wall, a technician was rearranging vials marked with a skull and crossbones.

"As might guess, area contain virus stockpile." Natasha motioned to the right and continued, "And here vaccine. At present, we have supply in building to inoculate million people.

"How much virus?" he asked.

"Oh, much less. Even one dose wipe out world. Except people vaccinated."

Aaron noticed that frost crept across the glass of the vaccine room door. He reached out to touch the surface.

Natasha said, "Can tell not quite airtight, but close enough for purpose. We keep vaccine minus ten degree Celsius or it degrade. Once vaccine exposed to higher temperature we believe survive only twelve, thirteen, maybe twenty-four hour. Not sure. We not infect anyone, give vaccine after more than one day old to know. Not right."

She plans to kill millions of Americans and Jews, but it wouldn't be right to subject a guinea pig to a vaccine older than a day. . . . Interesting.

Aaron forced a blank expression to disguise his disgust.

They walked down the long corridor until they came upon a sitting area with a small round table and four chairs. A coffee pot sat on a counter against one wall and several small cups were laid out around a samovar. A young Asian man was seated at the table. He stood and gave a half bow to Dr. Borisova.

"This Kim," she said to Aaron.

"Good morning," Aaron said, smiling and extending his hand.

Borisova pushed his hand away and snapped. "Korean. Not speak English."

Judging from the cheap suit, he must be North Korean. The ill-fitting suit was at least twenty years out of date. Aaron could also discern broad shoulders, thick biceps, and a lean frame underneath. *Wonder if he's a visiting scientist. Or is there some other reason he's here?* He continued to smile and nodded.

"I notice he isn't wearing protective clothing. Is he a scientist as well?" Aaron turned to view Borisova's reaction.

"No, he like you, assassin. May change plan. Understand Americans believe China create COVID virus. So borrow Kim, from friends in North Korea. Might replace you." She lowered her eyelids and smiled.

TWENTY

White House

"Mr. President." Steve Simpson stood in the Oval Office doorway. His boss looked up from the Resolute Desk at his call.

"Yeah, Steve, what's up?"

"Sir, I had an idea about the upcoming G-7 meeting." Steve paused but pushed on before the president could weigh in on the subject. "We're still hearing a lot of Israeli chatter that the Rus—, excuse me, that someone is looking to unleash a new coronavirus."

"Steve, what did I tell you? You can't trust the Israelis. They've got something up their sleeve. Now, if that's all you got, turn around and get the hell out."

"But, sir, please let me finish." This time he paused and awaited approval.

Parker sneered but waved him on.

"The ambassadors from three of the G-7 participants have already raised concerns about holding the meeting right now."

"Goddamn it." Parker slammed both hands on the desk. "Those idiots. What cowards. We're not going to cancel because the Jews are spewing lies. I won't have it. Get their leaders on the phone. I'll fix this."

"Sir, before you go any further, I have an idea that I think will resolve this and address another problem."

The crimson in Parker's cheeks paled a tad, and he motioned at Steve to continue.

"Perhaps it would be wise to relocate the G-7 meeting to Camp David. In the, um, unlikely event that the Israelis are correct. It would be far easier to minimize any threat to the world leaders by holding the meeting there. And," Steve grinned, "holding the event there would be a perfect excuse to close off the rest of Catoctin Mountain Park surrounding Camp David. And," he pointed a finger skyward, "you could even clear-cut some of the forest around the camp to enhance security. If you catch my drift."

Parker smiled and leaned back in his chair. "Hmm. Very interesting, Steve. Very interesting. Perhaps Camp David would be a . . . prudent solution. I mean, given the threat and all."

"Yes, sir. I think you're exactly right. It would be prudent. And who's to say we shouldn't keep the park closed to enhance security at the president's retreat? And then, perhaps, we can give the Congress more details of our new plan to upgrade security at the camp for COG. In fact, we might even need supplemental appropriations, for national security, of course. With your permission, I'll have OMB director O'Keefe begin planning a request for funds to enhance national security. It's probably too late to get it in the current CR, but knowing the Congress, there will be another one before they conclude for the year."

Parker waved his acquiescence.

Steve offered a little bow, excusing himself. *Well, that went perfectly. I've got the solution for his golf course and a better way to secure the G-7 meeting. Think I've earned my salary today.*

But he still had no way to foil the Russians.

TWENTY-ONE

ROLL CALL

SENATE SPENDING PANEL ACTS TO STAVE OFF SHUTDOWN
By Harris Ward, Washington, DC

The Senate Committee on Appropriations reported a short-term spending bill today that will keep government's lights on for the next eight weeks. Absent this measure, which still must be passed by the full Senate and signed by the president, the government would be forced to shut down next Monday with the advent of the new fiscal year.

The passage of such bills—a continuing resolution in Washington parlance—has become an annual ritual in the budget process. In recent decades Congress has struggled to meet its self-imposed deadline of passing its appropriations bills by September 30.

Tuesday's meeting of the Senate Appropriations Committee was odd in that such routine measures rarely require the formal approval of the committee before being considered by the full Senate. The measure already passed the House of Representatives by a nearly unanimous vote. According to unnamed committee sources, the minority Republicans insisted that the Senate Appropriations Committee meet to approve the short-term spending bill.

Notably absent from the committee meeting was Chairman Harry

Lackland of Virginia. Elizabeth Boyer, the junior senator from California, announced that Senator Lackland was tending to a family matter in southern Virginia. *Roll Call* noted a look of surprise from several meeting participants as Boyer took center stage. No other explanation was offered for the chairman's absence. Committee sources offered no timeline for when Chairman Lackland may return.

According to one senator, who refused to be identified, Senator Lackland has not been seen in the Capitol since the Senate returned from its summer break. Rumor has it that he did meet with at least one member during that time.

Senator Boyer gaveled the committee to order and quickly moved toward passage of the bill. The committee also adopted new subcommittee spending allocations. According to a committee spokesperson, the new allocation measure will pave the way for the completion of the appropriations bill for the Department of Defense, a bill Boyer helped draft as chair of the Defense Subcommittee.

There is every indication that the president will approve the legislation when it reaches his desk.

TWENTY-TWO

Oahu, Hawaii

"Captain Ong, sir, you got a minute?" Paul Hackett asked upon entering the head shed—the boss's office—at the new NSA facility on Oahu.

Technical Sergeant Amy Anderson, trailing behind her civilian supervisor, glanced around the space. It was her first time in the commander's office since the outpost had relocated from the old pineapple plantation. This was way nicer than the leaky underground World War II airplane manufacturing facility that had housed the secretive agency for the last half of the twentieth century.

The captain looked up and motioned them forward. Amy studied the navy captain's face, concerned that he might blanch when he saw she was the one accompanying Mr. Hackett. He flinched slightly when their eyes met, his behind coke-bottle lenses and hers, bright green under short red curls. His gaze resting on her, his dispassionate demeanor quickly returned.

"Sergeant Anderson, this is the first time I've seen you since your return to Hawaii. Everything going okay?" Captain Ong asked.

Amy nodded, but her jaw was clamped tight. "Yes, sir, thank you, sir." She forced a smile.

"Good. What can I do for you Paul . . . and Amy?"

"Sir, you obviously know Sergeant Anderson," Mr. Hackett offered, gesturing to Amy.

"Only by reputation." Captain Ong chuckled. "In any other business, our technical sergeant, here, would probably be famous—or infamous in some circles. I hope you aren't here to add to that fame, Paul?"

"No, sir." Mr. Hackett shook his head. "But Sergeant Anderson—Amy—has some intel that I believe you need to see immediately."

"Sergeant?" Captain Ong's eyes shifted to her.

"Yes, sir. First, let me say thank you for welcoming me back. I'm sure you were warned about me because of the incident in DC." Amy offered a timid smile.

"Indeed I was. But I've also been told you're a brilliant analyst. Your methods might have been, shall we say, unconventional. But your previous supervisors vouch for you, saying you always act with the good of the nation as your compass." The captain's tone was absent of emotion.

"Yes, sir. Thanks, again." Amy continued, "Captain, I've been monitoring signals from North Korea and matching them with chatter from South Korean human sources. It's pretty clear the North is working with the Russians on what sounds like a bioweapon. We don't know more details, how or where, but it seems like they intend to infect the West, with the US as the primary target."

"Oh, sweet Jesus." Ong frowned. "We've had that corroborated by a sister service but have been told to stand down."

Mr. Hackett cocked his head. "Stand down. Why? If Amy's intel is accurate, we could be facing a very serious threat, and if it's already been reported, well, doesn't that corroborate her info? We can't ignore it.

Can we, Captain?" The urgency in Hackett's voice was perceptible.

Captain Ong removed his glasses and wiped his face with both hands. "Listen, this can't leave this room. The Israelis have been reporting similar intel. But they aren't considered credible sources. Headquarters says the White House has banned anyone from talking about this development."

"That's crazy!" Mr. Hackett almost shouted.

Captain Ong held up one hand. "I know, Paul. But the commander in chief is telling us to stand down. That's a direct order."

Amy's posture sagged. *Not again. Why do these things always happen to me? That's the same guy who wanted to rig that election. And I think he did. It just didn't work out the way he wanted.*

"Understood, Captain." Mr. Hackett stiffened his spine. "But if the nation is under attack, we have to defend her."

Captain Ong replaced his glasses, paused for a moment and frowned. "Sergeant Anderson, let me be very clear. I am not and would never authorize leaking of classified material. In your previous actions, you talked to cleared individuals on the Hill. That is not allowed under our regulations. It is a gray area under the whistleblower statute, probably the reason you're here and not in Leavenworth. Can you fill us in on that earlier incident?"

Amy released a huge breath. Using as few words as possible, she quickly told how she'd informed the clerk of the Senate's Defense Appropriations Subcommittee about the plan to rig elections and how the rest of that story unfolded. At the end, she added, "But the staffer I know, um, knew, Fred Hendricks, he retired, sir. I don't think we can tell him about this."

"That's quite a story. And you're sure President Parker was behind the whole thing?"

"No, sir. I can't say that with certainty. But I know that's what Mister Fred, um, Mr. Hendricks, thought."

"Sir," Mr. Hackett interrupted, a note of hope in his voice, "perhaps there is a way." He motioned to a chair and the captain signaled for the two of them to sit.

TWENTY-THREE

The Capitol

Senator Liz Boyer from California affixed the microphone to her light blue blazer. From behind the majority leader's desk, the spot reserved for the senator managing the pending legislation in the Senate, she addressed the presiding officer who sat atop the dais, "Madam President."

The presiding officer, today the junior senator from Illinois, a youngish African American woman with the sweetest smile, glanced down at the Senate parliamentarian for instructions and then spoke. "The senator from California is recognized." As was customary, the role of presiding officer was filled by one of a rotating group of freshman senators tasked with presiding over the Senate for an hour at a time in the absence of the vice president of the United States or the second-highest-ranking official, the senior senator of the majority party who was designated the president pro tempore.

"Thank you, Madam President," Liz said. "What is the pending business before the Senate?"

"Under the previous order, morning business is closed and House joint resolution 143 is the pending business," the presiding officer read from the script that the parliamentarian had prepared. She smiled again and nodded in Liz's direction.

"Thank you, Madam President," Liz began. "On behalf of Chairman Lackland, who has been unavoidably detained this morning, I want to inform all members that it is vital that the Senate pass this bill today before we adjourn for the week. The bill is virtually the same bill as was passed by the House last week. It provides continued funding of government operations for the next eight weeks as the House and Senate work to address our differences in conference on our twelve appropriations bills."

"Would the senator yield for a question?" called out a middle-aged man with curly brown hair and an angular face from the other side of the chamber.

Liz turned her head in the gentleman's direction and frowned. "Not at this moment, but it won't take me long to conclude my statement. If the senator from Tennessee wouldn't mind." She tried to smile, but it must have come out as a grimace.

"But, Madam President," he cried, "renewing my request, the senator from California implied that twelve appropriations bills were in conference. It is my understanding that only one bill has passed both chambers and is in conference. And—"

The presiding officer tapped her gavel and spoke sternly. "The senator will refrain. The senator from California has the floor." She nodded again to Liz.

"Thank you, Madam President." Liz flashed a look at Senator George of Tennessee and continued. "Again, without action on this legislation today, the government will cease to have funding for its operations beginning on Monday. This is a very noncontroversial measure. Even in these hyperpartisan times, the bill passed the House by an overwhelming vote. Frankly, that shouldn't be surprising. None of my colleagues seek to shut down government operations. It's bad policy and bad politics. We've all learned that the hard way from past shutdowns. They are costly. They wreak havoc on the executive branch, for everything from the military and highway repair to support for our farmers and operations at the national laboratories, including the one in Oak Ridge, Tennessee."

Liz glanced again at Senator George. She couldn't help but smirk as she paused and took a long, slow sip of water.

"Madam President," she continued, "there is no reason to wait any longer. I ask for third reading."

"Is there further debate on the measure?" The presiding officer scanned the chamber. Other than a handful of staffers seated at the back and the Senate floor staff near the dais, the only senators in the chamber were the three of them.

Senator George stood up and reached for his microphone. Pat Sistrunk, who had been watching the proceedings from the back of the chamber, came bounding down the aisle. He was spitting words at Liz. "Quorum call! Quorum call!"

She blurted out, "I suggest the absence of a quorum."

Senator George raised his microphone and inquired, "Would the senator withhold that request?"

Sistrunk waved his arms violently at Liz, and she repeated in a louder voice, "Madam President, I suggest the absence of a quorum." She glared first at Sistrunk and then at Senator George.

"The clerk will call the roll to denote the presence of a quorum." The presiding officer banged the gavel once.

Senator George removed his microphone and slammed it in its holder. He turned and stomped up the steps toward the back of the chamber. Pointing in the direction of Pat Sistrunk, Liz saw him bite the head off of his staffer who handled appropriations matters. "Who the hell is that guy?" she heard him roar.

Before the staffer could respond, Senator George grabbed the elbow of the Republican minority leader's chief staffer on the floor as she passed by him.

"Senator George," the thin blonde woman said wearily, "that *guy* is Pat Sistrunk. He's Senator Lackland's staff director of the Appropriations Committee."

"Yeah, so what? Who does he think he is, the hundred and first senator?"

TWENTY-FOUR

NSA Facility, Wahiawa, Oahu

"Is this Mister Fred?"

"Ha," Fred Hendricks purred into his cell, "only one person calls me that. Amy Anderson, how are you? Or should I say, 'aloha'? Heard you were back in Hawaii."

"Aloha! And loving it. How 'bout you? Still enjoying your golden years on the river in Maryland? Ever get that boat fixed? Or are you still sitting around, drinking Maker's Mark and that flying squirrel beer, and thinking about it?"

"You got me pegged. It's good to hear your voice, Amy. I'm loving life. No complaints. Although it's a bit quieter since you left town. Haven't seen your cousin around."

Amy could detect the wink accompanying that statement and she felt her green eyes fill with fire. She'd never forgotten the last time she had seen Fred, when her cousin Rachel was so obviously flirting with him and flaunting her curves. But Amy put it out of her mind and turned quickly to the much more serious subject at hand. "So, Fred, I'd love to chat, but I got a favor to ask."

"Shoot, Amy."

"Okay, so, you know how I keep getting mixed up in these, um, things, like when you and I met?" Her index finger twirled an Orphan Annie curl as she spoke.

"Yeah?" Fred's low growl contained quizzical notes.

"Well, it's happening again."

"Jesus Christ, Amy. What now? And why are you talking to me? Didn't the last episode teach you? You got to go through channels." She imagined him shaking his head as he spoke.

"Actually, I'm talking to you at the direction of my CO, a navy captain. He wanted to make sure some info got passed to the Hill, but didn't know how."

"Okay, stop right there. You know I don't work on the committee anymore. And I don't have a security clearance any longer. And you know better than to talk about classified stuff over the phone." He sounded like a dad admonishing his teenage daughter.

"Hey, Fred. Wait a second." Amy's voice was louder and edgier. "What do you take me for? First, I know you're retired. Second, do you think I'd ever talk about classified stuff on the phone? Did you forget who I work for? If there's anybody sensitive to saying stuff on nonsecure lines, you can be sure it's me. I'm not authorized to tell you anything classified. But my boss wants something to get passed on. And it's serious or I wouldn't be calling."

"All right, sorry. But after last time, I wondered if you'd forgotten all those guys in black SUVs coming after us. I never thought you'd be talking to me about that kind of stuff again."

An apologetic tone and that purr she'd found so attractive replaced his growl. She smiled and thought back to those days during and after the ordeal.

"So, what's this about, Amy?"

TWENTY-FIVE

The Capitol

"What the hell is going on? A quorum call? And why is Liz Boyer managing the bill? Where the fuck is Harry, Pat?" The majority leader's angry voice came shouting through the phone.

"Chairman Lackland was unable to be here this morning, Senator Johnson, and since the bill has to be passed today, I asked Senator Boyer to manage." Pat Sistrunk was standing in the busy hallway next to the Senate chamber. He felt surprisingly calm even though he could feel the majority leader's rage. Having dodged a few bullets by having Senator Boyer mark up the CR, and now getting the quorum call before Senator George could cause any mischief, Pat sensed a winning streak.

"What do you mean he's not here? Why not? And don't go saying it's a personal matter."

"Um, sorry, sir. But I think you need to ask his wife, Beverly. She's the only one—"

"I'm asking you, Pat. Beverly isn't taking my calls. She doesn't work for the Senate. You do. And, if you like your job, I'd suggest you answer the fucking question."

Oh boy. What do I do?

It was his job to protect the chairman, and Mrs. Lackland would kill him if he said anything about the chairman's condition, but this was the majority leader.

I'm not sure what's right. It's pretty clear Lackland isn't up to the job. An uncomfortable silence dragged on.

"Listen, Pat." Charley Johnson's voice had dropped a couple notches to a near whisper. Pat wasn't sure if he was calming down or about to explode.

"I understand you want to protect Harry. And that's admirable. But he's the chairman of the Appropriations Committee and he's got a bill on the floor. And it's my job to run the Senate, so I need to know. I promise I won't pass on any details. What's wrong with him?"

Pat released a long, heavy sigh and ducked into a corner away from the tourists, lobbyists, and other congressional employees. He whispered, "Senator, Chairman Lackland had a stroke."

"What? When?"

Pat checked over both shoulders making sure no one was listening in. "At the beginning of the August break."

"Is he okay?"

"No, sir, he's not." Pat's lower lip trembled and he wiped away a tear. "He's in a bad way and it's been almost eight weeks. And Beverly isn't letting anyone see him. She realizes he's not capable of . . . Senator, he can't talk. I don't think he's aware of where he is or what's going on around him. He's alive, but that's about all."

"Holy mother of God. Oh, Pat, that's terrible. Are the doctors offering any hope?"

"Right after it happened, the doctor at Walter Reed was pretty blunt that Senator Lackland most certainly won't recover. That's all I know. Only Mrs. Lackland would know more."

"Oh, dear. He'll have to resign. Do you know what that means?"

"Well, I guess so. The governor of Virginia will appoint someone to replace him."

"Pat, it means the Senate flips. We have a 51–49 majority. If Harry dies, or resigns, the *Republican* governor of Virginia will appoint a Republican. That's 50–50. *Republican* Vice President Sanchez breaks the ties. They're in charge and we're back in the minority. Jesus Christ, Pat. Could it get any worse?" The line went quiet for a moment. Pat thought the leader might have hung up on him as he usually did. Then Johnson spoke, "Okay, for now, this stays between the two of us. We have to get this bill done. Jacobs promised me no shenanigans from the minority. So, why did Boyer put us into a quorum call?"

Pat was struggling to make sense of it all. And it finally dawned on him. The leader was right. If Lackland couldn't continue . . . Mrs. Lackland hadn't probably considered that when she insisted no one know about the chairman. But the leader had asked a question about the bill that demanded a response. "Yes, sir. My minority counterpart told me that George, um, Senator George, sir, wanted to offer an amendment to cut the CR by five percent. Your staff and mine believed the bill had no opposition. Since we didn't know if that would open the floodgates to more amendments, the smart people on my staff suggested we call for a quorum.

"They suggested that you might want to fill the amendment tree to stop George from offering his amendment, and then you can negotiate a deal with the Republicans."

"That son of a bitch is such an impediment. I wish the people of Tennessee could see what a jackass he is. Why didn't you tell me, Pat?"

"Sir, I called your staff, but they didn't call me back."

"Alright. I'll have my staff write up the script and talk to Jacobs about working out an agreement. He promised me we'd get this done today. We all know George won't win a vote, but we can't allow him to talk the bill to death. My colleagues will kill me if we have to stay around this weekend to satisfy that idiot. Give me thirty minutes and meet me on the floor."

"Yes, sir."

"And not a word to anyone about Harry."

TWENTY-SIX

Dirksen Senate Office Building

Larraine Walker, the longtime clerical staffer on the Defense Subcommittee, hammered excitedly on Paula's opened door. The chubby gray-haired woman was beaming.

"Paula, Fred Hendricks is here!" She was bouncing on her toes and her voice was nearly an octave higher than normal.

"Fred's here? Well, please send him in." Paula's voice was as merry as Larraine's demeanor.

The former Senate staffer and clerk of the Defense Subcommittee limped into the room. Fred was something of an éminence grise from his forty years of service to both parties. "Wow, you look great, Paula. Welcome back." He glanced around at the new artwork adorning the walls. Everything else was as he'd left it three years earlier. "I heard you married Chauncey Hayes and were living the dream in Hawaii. Can't believe you're here. How is Chauncey? Did I hear you have twins?"

Paula plucked a framed photo from her desk and walked over to where the older man was standing smiling. His penetrating gray eyes stood out from his deeply lined face. Paula handed him the picture. "My boys. You know Chauncey, and that's Charlie on the left and his younger brother Ross. A full five minutes younger."

"Cute." Fred handed the picture back and looked her over. "You look the same. Still as gorgeous as ever."

Paula felt herself blush and clutched the picture to her chest. "How are you, Fred? Enjoying retirement?" She paused and scrunched up her nose. "I have to know. How are you passing the time? I mean, I heard you just quit it all. No lobbying, no—what?—teaching, no think tank or anything?"

Fred shook his head but couldn't shake the smile. "Nope. None. A little fishing, reading, working on my boat. After forty years here, I'm taking it easy. It's all good."

"Wow. I'm not sure I could do that. But if it works for you, that's terrific. I'm so glad you stopped in. What's up?"

"Actually, a friend contacted me and asked me to talk to you."

"Oh? Looking for a job or something?"

"Nah, nothing like that." Fred looked back at the open doorway and lowered his voice to that familiar purr. "She thought it was urgent, so I drove right over. I hope I'm not bothering you. It's kinda sensitive. Can I close the door?"

"Sure." Paula, curious, motioned for him to go ahead.

His foot snapped the door stop and the reception area door swung shut.

"So, what's up?" She replaced the picture on her desk, turned, and leaned against the deep wooden top. She motioned to the chairs in front of her desk. "Do you want to sit?"

Fred shook his head. "I'll only be a minute." He lowered his voice again. "Did Stevie Guy brief you about our little escapade with the White House that happened right before I retired?"

"Oh my gosh, yeah. He gave me a few details." Paula's eyes widened. "Don't tell me they're at it again."

Fred raised his hands palms out and shook his head. "Well, not that I know. But the gal who told me about that whole mess is the one who just called me. She's in Hawaii now."

"Well, lucky her."

"Hah, yeah. She's an air force sergeant, cyber expert assigned to the NSA. She couldn't go into much detail since I'm no longer cleared. What I can deduce is that they believe the Russians are working with the North Koreans on a bioweapon. Her boss wanted to make sure someone up here knew and could check it out. She implied the White House is trying to quash the story. Like I said, she couldn't tell me much. I figured you and Stevie and whoever else you got working that stuff could sniff around."

"Huh." Paula looked up and exhaled a deep breath toward the ceiling. Her eyes narrowed as she looked back at Fred. "Well, you know I can't really comment on the issue, but I will say you're the second person who's mentioned something like this. Sounds like we'll have to do some more digging."

"I think that would be good. Amy, uh, the air force sergeant, said her people are pretty spun up about it. But their hands are tied."

Paula looked up as someone rapped on the other doorway leading to the staff offices. "Yes?"

Mindy Abrams stuck her head in. "Boss, the CR . . ." Her eyes moved to Paula's guest. "Fred Hendricks! Good Lord! Wow, you look relaxed. How are you?" She glanced back at Paula. "Oh, sorry, boss. I just . . ."

"No problem, Mindy. What's up?"

"Yes, ma'am. The leader's on the floor. He's calling the CR back up."

Paula switched on her TV as the presiding officer recognized the majority leader. "Sorry, Fred. Duty calls. You want to grab a seat? It'll be like old times."

Fred Hendricks pursed his lips and shook his head. "No, thank you. I'm already getting the shakes being here this long."

Mindy snorted, and Paula nodded, settling herself into her desk chair.

"Listen, Paula, that's all I wanted to say, so I'll leave you and Mindy to monitor the floor proceedings." He winked at her. "But, Mindy?" He wagged a finger. "You better be on your best behavior or Paula'll cut off your beer supply." He winked again, gave a wave, and walked out into the reception area.

The majority leader offered first- and second-degree amendments along with a confusing assortment of motions that effectively precluded any senator from offering any other amendment without the approval of all senators. Johnson spied Senator George coming through the door, nodded in his direction, and spoke again. "Mr. President?"

From his perch on top of the dais, the junior senator from Oregon and newest member of the Senate called on the leader.

"Thank you, Mr. President. I see the junior senator from Tennessee is on the floor and, with that, I have a unanimous consent to propound." He paused to survey the scene. The minority leader, Senator Jacobs, pushed through the heavy glass, brass, and wood doors at the rear of the chamber and gave him a thumbs-up.

Senator Johnson spoke again. "I ask unanimous consent that all pending amendments and motions be withdrawn, that the senator from Tennessee be recognized at . . ." he glanced up at the clock. The time was 11:13 a.m. "Eleven fifteen a.m. to offer amendment number 1755, that there be twenty minutes of debate on the amendment equally divided in the usual form, that no second-degree or perfecting amendments be in order, and that upon the conclusion of the debate, the Senate vote on or in relation to the amendment. I ask further that, upon disposition of the amendment, the bill be read for a third time and the Senate proceed to final passage without any intervening action or debate." Johnson looked up from the script in the direction of the chair.

The presiding officer leaned forward, listening to the instructions of the assistant parliamentarian, who was positioned below and to his right. Then he sat up straight and spoke into the microphone. "Is there objection to the request?" He paused to look at the senator from Tennessee and then over at the minority leader, who had proceeded down the steps and was standing at his desk across the aisle from the majority leader.

Senator George grabbed a microphone from a desk in the last row of the chamber and spoke. "Reserving the right to object . . ."

An audible groan arose from both Republican and Democratic staff seated in the Byrd cages. The murmured rumble started to swell from those same staff seating areas in the two corners at the rear of the chamber.

The presiding officer banged his gavel sharply and said, "The Senate will come to order. Please take any conversations off the floor. The senator from Tennessee is recognized."

Senator George nodded. "Thank you, Mr. President. As I said, reserving the right to object, could the leader explain why this consent is necessary? Why should the Senate be limited to offering only a single amendment on this bill which allows the government to spend countless hundreds of billions of dollars of money that we don't have? The national debt is swelling every minute of every day. Yet this body wants to continue to write bad checks. I am outraged—"

The presiding officer listened to the parliamentarian. He tapped his gavel and glared at Senator George. "Does the senator object to the request?"

The majority leader interrupted. "Mr. President, renewing my request, let me add that everyone in America knows that we need to pass this bill today so our government can continue to function. It is the responsibility of leaders in this body to ensure that a shutdown does not occur. Now, I could offer a motion to cut off debate on the bill without any—*any*—amendments," the leader shouted and slammed the script onto his desk. "And we could all sit here for two days, with a cloture vote at one minute after midnight on Sunday morning, and then a vote on final passage on Monday. If any senator objects to this request, that is *EXACTLY*," he bellowed and jabbed his index finger into his desk, "*exactly* what we're going to do. Just so everyone is aware."

The leader looked around the room. A half dozen of his colleagues had entered the floor and were milling about. Several were wearing sport coats and khaki trousers instead of the normal business suits. They were carrying coats and briefcases, anticipating a trip to National Airport as soon as the bill passed. Senator Jacobs had walked over to Senator George. He covered the junior senator's microphone with his hand and whispered in his ear.

"Mr. President, I renew my request," the leader insisted.

The parliamentarian had replaced her assistant. She whispered instructions to the presiding officer, who said, "Is there objection to the request?" He stared at Senator George.

Senator George sat down, with Jacobs leaning over him.

"Without objection, the request is agreed to." The presiding officer banged the gavel. "The hour of eleven fifteen having arrived, the senator from Tennessee is recognized to offer amendment number 1755." He pounded his gavel several times as if daring anyone to challenge the ruling.

"Wow, Paula, that was a close one." Mindy had helped herself to one of the two chairs in front of Paula's partners desk. She sat slouched with her feet resting on the secretary's notetaking panel jutting from the front of Paula's desk.

"Yeah, Senator George is being a jerk, like always. It's all for show. He knows the leader would've run out the clock if he objected. It's just a way for him to continue his quixotic quest to mess things up."

"It's times like these I wish they had killed the filibuster," Mindy said. "I mean, we wouldn't have to sit here all weekend. Johnson could've passed the bill without having to rely on minority cooperation."

"I'm not so sure, Mindy. Even if we eliminated the sixty-vote threshold, the Senate still requires unlimited debate before you can vote on a bill. If the leader had tried to ram this through without support from the minority, I bet George would've been joined by a dozen or so Republicans. They would've spoken for hours and tried to offer dozens of amendments through unanimous consent requests. Even if the leader had the votes—or even if he had sixty votes—the Senate would still be stuck here for the weekend burning up the cloture time. And members would be hacked off at each other, and both sides would be blaming the other for the delay. And our CR, which everyone but George wants to pass, would be hung up. Doesn't sound like progress to me."

"I guess, but the filibuster sure ain't democracy. Why should a minority get to tell the majority no? That doesn't sound very American to me."

"Fair point. But I think it's all part of this complicated system of checks and balances. The House is based on one person, one vote. The

White House is all about one guy telling the rest of us what we can and can't do. And the Supreme Court is supposed to be the safeguard when somebody tries to go too far. But the Senate is a hybrid. It's supposed to protect states' rights, particularly those of the little states. Don't forget, originally senators weren't elected. They were selected by state legislators. I think they were supposed to be a check on the people's house, where members are all elected by majority vote. The House is supposed to reflect popular sentiment even when it might not be in the best interest of the country. What some call the tyranny of the majority or the masses. The Senate was set up to ensure minority rights. The House is all about majority rights. It's like yin and yang."

"But there ain't nothing in the Constitution about filibusters. And the rules have been changed before."

"You're quite right. And if both parties thought they should eliminate the filibuster, I suppose I'd acquiesce, but I still think it would be bad for public policy. Compromise is almost always a good thing. And what's really bad is when one side wants to change the rules and the other side doesn't and the party in the majority says, 'We're doing it anyway.' That's about as unsenatorial and undemocratic as you can get."

TWENTY-SEVEN

Yekaterinburg

Aaron straightened his leather jacket, ran his fingers through his hair, knocked on the apartment door, and took a step back. After a moment the door cracked open and Natasha Borisova peeked out.

"What you do here?" Her eyes were wide.

Aaron smiled and lifted a bottle of vodka toward the opening. "I'm sorry to bother you, but I wanted to talk. Plus, I don't like to drink alone. May I come in?"

She started to open the door and stopped. "How you find me?"

He smiled again and shrugged. "I followed you, yesterday. I thought maybe we could relax together sometime, seeing as we're colleagues, and I don't know anyone else. Besides, I didn't think it would be good for security to be seen in public together. So, I thought this was best. I hope that's okay?"

She glanced down at the bottle and sneered. "Muslim no drink alcohol."

He laughed. "Muslims aren't supposed to drink, but some do. Especially those of us who spend time in the West wooing rich Americans and Europeans out of their money."

She haltingly opened the door and stood aside for him to pass.

"Well, you not woo this Russian."

"Absolutely not. As I said. I just wanted to talk. And," he held up the bottle, "I've found this to be a good icebreaker."

He looked around the small white-walled apartment. A tiny kitchen off to the left, a two-person dining table wedged in an alcove, the small living room crammed with a couch, coffee table, one comfortable chair, and TV. To the right he could see into the bedroom, where a double bed dominated the space. Sparse. But his eye did catch on a red negligee lying on the bed. A splash of color and, dare say, luxury in the drab surroundings.

Natasha grabbed two shot glasses from a kitchen cabinet and closed the bedroom door on her way into the living space. She motioned for him to sit on the couch. He placed the bottle on the coffee table and sat. Natasha took the chair.

Aaron poured two shots and raised his glass. "*Na zdorov'ye.*"

Natasha chuckled and clinked his glass. "Cheers." She took a sip. "I not suppose Arabs make toast."

Aaron shook his head. "Alcohol toasts are not appropriate for Muslims, of course. But we Arabs have many toasts for food. To health. Good luck, and others."

He threw back the shot. With a smile, Natasha followed. Her cheeks flushed with the hit of eighty-proof alcohol. He poured a second for them both. He downed it and placed his glass on the table with a loud clunk.

Natasha laughed. "You sure not part Russian? *Do dna!* To the bottom!" She drained her glass and placed it on the table without a sound.

He refilled their glasses, but before he could raise his, Natasha placed her hand on his forearm. "What talk about? We go like this, we not able." A thin smile curved her lips, but her eyes held a wariness.

Aaron leaned back on the couch and looked around the room. "Is it safe to speak, um, freely?"

"Yes, of course. Why no?"

"They say walls have ears. Perhaps the Americans, the Chinese, or maybe North Koreans?"

"Don't be silly. No one listen. What?"

He scooted forward on the couch. "Let me assume that our target would be a high-level meeting or gathering of important officials. One, I assume, that Russia would not be a party to. Perhaps like the upcoming G-7 meeting." He cocked his head and raised his eyebrows with a hint of a smile.

Dr. Borisova chuckled. "And if, so what?"

"Well, then, Kim would be useless."

"Why? He skilled. Fit in. Many Asians in US. Washington cosmopolitan. You must know."

"Of course. But the meeting won't be in Washington. The location has been changed. It will be at a military base called Camp David, which is ninety kilometers away. The camp has served as a presidential retreat for eighty years. It's in the middle of a forest and will be surrounded by security. How would someone, who doesn't even speak English, get close enough to the participants to infect them? Are you going to pretend he's a mute?" He scoffed.

Her cheeks lost the alcohol bloom. Her posture stiffened and the muscles in her shoulders tightened. "How you know?" she snapped.

"I read it on the internet and I checked with a friend in the US, who confirmed it." He downed his third shot and raised the empty glass in her direction. She picked up her shot and, after holding it for a moment, followed suit.

"If correct, and plan attack summit, would be problem. But now, not problem." She shrugged, but her face remained drained of color. "You know soon."

Aaron leaned back against the couch and stared at her. After a moment, he scooted forward on the couch again. "Good then. Let's drink to our success." He poured two more shots.

"I think try get me drunk. Not know cannot outdrink Russian?" She threw down the shot and stood up. "Now, time you go."

Aaron looked at the vodka. "But the bottle is still half full. What's the rush?"

"Have early morning. You leave." She waved her hand toward the door.

He stood up and stepped in front of her. Close enough to touch lips, he whispered, "Are you sure I should go?" He stared into her eyes. He sensed she might be wondering the same thing.

Natasha gasped softly and took a quick step backward, nearly stumbling into the chair. She stood up straighter and inhaled deeply. "Yes, sure. Good night." She motioned with an index finger toward the door.

Aaron offered a slight bow. "Very well, then, madam. I won't keep you any longer." He turned and opened the door. Natasha followed him across the room. He spun around, finding himself again only inches away from her, and placed one hand on her hip. "Perhaps we can do this again." She stepped back and he smiled. "We still have half a bottle." She opened her mouth to speak, but he spun around and walked out, closing the door behind him.

He zipped his leather jacket and turned up his collar. *That went well. Even though she didn't admit they are targeting the G-7. Next time.* He chuckled and went shivering into the frigid night air.

TWENTY-EIGHT

October

White House

"Mr. President." Steve Simpson sped into the Oval Office without knocking and rushed over to change the TV channel from a golf tournament to CNN.

"What the hell are you doing?" President Parker leaned forward in his chair and snarled. "I was watching that."

Steve backed away from the TV without a word.

CNN newsman Zack Trap appeared on the screen following the red and gold breaking news banner. Trap's excited voice began, "A shocking new video was released today from a group calling itself the Anti-Imperialist Society. The graphic film has been sanitized by CNN. It shows the bodies and horrific deaths of peasants in a small hamlet in eastern Kazakhstan said to have been caused by a new deadly coronavirus that causes respiratory failure. Please note the following video may not be suitable for children."

The film with Trap's voiceover showed a dozen dead bodies of what looked like peasant farmers lined up on the ground. "The group releasing the video warned Western nations. Unless they meet its demands to remove all foreign troops from Asia, the Middle East, and

Eastern Europe, it will release a new coronavirus in the capital cities of Western Europe and the United States in ten days. They claim the virus is ten times deadlier that COVID-19. CNN is unable to verify the video. It is unaware of the group claiming credit—or perhaps blame is a better descriptor—for this new coronavirus."

"Jesus Christ, Steve. If this is accurate. Those goddamn Chinese. Where is this place?"

"Sir, it's an eastern corner of Kazakhstan, right across the Russian and Chinese borders. As they are saying, they can't confirm the veracity of the report. But it sounds bad. Sir, this might confirm the warning from the Israelis about Russia."

"Russia? What the hell has this got to do with Russia? It's China, Steve. The China virus. Remember? Didn't you say it's on the border with China?"

"Yes, sir. But also very near the Russian border. And Russia is the country we believe may be developing a new coronavirus strain. So—"

"That's ridiculous. Russia wouldn't do this. It's China. Didn't they threaten us if we don't pull our troops out of Asia? Did you forget our troops are in South Korea and Japan?"

"No, sir, not to mention Singapore, some special operators in the Philippines, et cetera. But the film also said to remove troops in Europe. That's been a goal of Putin since he first took over. And all the intel suggests that Russia—"

"What did I tell you about Russia? That's enough. Get Defense Secretary Vest on the phone. We have to start planning a counterattack, maybe on that new Chinese naval base that's got the Taiwanese up in arms. We can't let them get away with this. Those bastards. I won't have the country back in lockdown over a new China virus."

"Yes, sir, but it's probably not China, sir. We have no evidence that China—"

"Have you gone deaf? No more. Start planning. Now!" Parker screamed and then continued in a moderated tone, "Maybe an amphibious assault. Take Hong Kong back."

"That's crazy . . ."

"Out of my office, and tell them to put the call through."

Steve threw up his hands and offered an exasperated, "Yes, sir, Mr. President," and departed.

TWENTY-NINE

Dirksen Senate Office Building

Paula was all alone in the committee's claustrophobic sensitive compartmented information facility down the hall from her office. She was sitting at a small desk in the vault surrounded by safes containing the nation's extremely sensitive defense and intelligence secrets. She picked up the secure phone and placed a call. "Hey, Al, it's Paula. How are you? How's the Asia Pacific Center? Still keeping the world safe for democracy?"

"Paula, it's so nice to hear from you. We miss you. I hope you're calling to tell me that you're coming home? That DC isn't what it once was and you want your old job back?"

Paula could sense a combination of whimsy and yet real interest in the booming voice of the retired three-star army general. Al Gianini was now the director of the Defense Department's Asia Pacific Center, a school dedicated to teaching Asian military and diplomatic leaders about democracy and civil-military relations. She imagined him sitting in his office, leaning back at his desk, admiring the swaying palm trees, bright blue skies, and open expanse of Fort DeRussy. The tiny army outpost was best known for its Hale Koa hotel, which provided rest and recreation for military personnel right smack in the middle of Waikiki.

"Al, something's up. Can you go secure?"

"Sure." She heard Al insert the key into his phone and they waited until the boxy black desk phone signaled it was okay to discuss classified information. Now they could discuss any information, from confidential to top secret, without fear of it being compromised. "Okay, I'm set. You?"

"All set here. So, I'm sure you heard about this new terrorist group with the bioweapon and the terrible slaughter at that village in Central Asia. Right?"

"Yes, horrific. Who'd do such a thing? And demanding we remove all our overseas forces. Don't they realize our military presence has been a stabilizing influence for the past seventy-five plus years? That's crazy talk. What do you know about it?"

"Oh, Al. It's making my head hurt. The scuttlebutt is the White House is churning up scenarios to make China pay."

"That might explain the late nights my military colleagues here in Hawaii are putting in. Our weekly three-star-and-up poker game got canceled last night. And that never happens. It's more sacrosanct than our Saturday morning tee time." He chuckled.

Paula could almost see her old boss's toothy grin. As the former deputy commander of the Pacific Command, now called the Indo-Pacific Command, all he could do was try to make light of this grave situation. "Okay. But here's the thing. What if I told you that the intelligence community is signaling that it is Russia behind the attack, not China? And I know for a fact that our Israeli allies think the same thing. And, finally, I heard from a former colleague that your NSA facility at Wahiawa thinks the North Koreans are involved, but involved with Russia, not China. Yet the administration is saber rattling with China."

"I'd say we got a problem. From the footage I saw, it looks like this is a real threat. If it's either China or Russia, we're extremely vulnerable. They're saying it's a coronavirus, but from what I've been reading, it reminds me of an anthrax attack. I mean, as terrible as COVID-19 was, it took days or even weeks after infection before it had compromised your respiratory system. But this sounds like it's a matter of a day or two. That's scary. And everyone who was exposed to it died. Even the young woman who lasted three days and talked to the hazmat doctor on the scene." Al paused. "But what's your involvement?"

"It's crazy. A few weeks ago, your good friend Senator Mitsunaga asked me to meet with an older Israeli man. I'm convinced the guy's Mossad even though the senator doesn't think so. Anyway, that guy said the Israelis had proof the Russians were planning to launch an engineered coronavirus against the US and Western Europe, and eventually Israel. The Israelis were begging the US to help them get ahold of the virus and a supposed antidote. But no one in our government would talk to them. Supposedly, the White House was burying their heads in the sand. But now, after this CNN report, they're going after China. It makes me want to pull out my hair and bay at the moon. And the Israelis want my help. But what the hell can I do?" Paula's voice rose with every word.

"Cripes, Paula. That's incredible. What a mess. And, if you're right and we're threatening China, we're back to where you and I were seven years ago after the incidents with North Korea. And that almost ended in all-out nuclear war."

"Don't remind me," she groaned. "Okay, so the reason I called you is to beg you to talk to PACOM or INDOPACOM. I guess that's the correct name now? I don't know the new four-star admiral and I don't have a Hawaii connection anymore. I thought he might listen to you, though. What's his name, Cooper?"

"Yeah, Dan Cooper. Submariner. Seems like a good guy. But I don't know him well. He's only been here for a month. I'll give him a call."

"One other idea." She paused, gathering her thoughts. "You still have that connection with the Chinese leadership? What was his name, Chen or something?"

"Vice Chairman Sheng. No. Unfortunately, he was, as they used to say, disappeared after the last change in party leadership. TV showed him being forcibly removed from a Communist Party meeting. So that connection has dried up."

"Shoot. I was hoping you could burn up the wires and see if we could help tamp this thing down." She stopped. "Hey, if you got any other ideas, I'm all ears. But I don't know what you or I can really do."

"What's your boss, your new chairman—is it Boyer?—what's she say?"

Paula scoffed. "Our relationship isn't mature enough for me to spring something like this on her. She's suspicious of both me and the Israelis. I told my supervisor, the committee's staff director who hired me, but he was useless. I don't know what else to do."

"Yeah, well, I'll call Admiral Cooper and see what I can do. But it'll probably be the same as with you and your boss. I haven't developed that kind of trust yet with this officer. I spring this on him and he might think I'm a crazy old Cold Warrior rattling my saber at the Iron Curtain. But I'll do what I can, Paula."

"Thanks, Al. Give my best to Midge."

"Will do. Take care of those little boys. And, Paula, your desk here is still empty when you decide it's time to return."

"You're sweet. Thanks." Paula hung up and groaned. She placed her head on the desktop and gently pounded it against the wooden surface.

THIRTY

The Capitol

Harris Ward spotted the junior California senator when she appeared in the doorway exiting the Senate chamber. He straightened his tortoiseshell eyeglasses, raised his digital recorder, and shouted, "Senator Boyer!" He squeezed through the throng of tourists and journalists who were awaiting the majority leader's anticipated exit from the chamber.

Liz Boyer heard her name and turned to see who it was. She frowned in apparent recognition that it was him, the *Roll Call* reporter.

He approached her and asked, "Excuse me, Senator, can I ask you a question?"

She sighed and nodded.

"Two weeks ago you replaced Chairman Lackland at the Appropriations Committee markup and last week you managed the bill on the floor." He gave her a wide smile. "Is there something we should know? Has there been a palace coup? Are you the new chairman?" He winked.

A smile broke across her face replacing the frown. "That's funny, Harris. Nope. No change. I'm still chairman of the Defense Subcommittee, and Harry Lackland's still our committee chairman. He asked that I substitute for him as he attended to some family matters."

"Oh, I see. So, what kind of family matters? What would keep him away from the Capitol for such a long time?" Harris probed. "From what I know, he wasn't here the entire month of September. Did he tell you why he's been absent?"

Boyer leaned away from him, her smile fading into a blank look. Harris was sure she was considering her response. Perhaps she hadn't realized the senator had been gone so long. Perhaps she knew exactly why and didn't want to say.

Harris broke the silence. "Senator, I've been covering Congress for more than forty years." He leaned a little closer and lowered his voice. "The last thing I want to do is speculate about someone's health. But when one of our oldest members is absent for a long period, it's natural for people to wonder if he is okay. People are beginning to talk. So, can you tell me what he said about his absence?" He tried to offer a sympathetic look. And, truthfully, he was concerned. Chairman Lackland was something of an institution in the body. His service predated that of Harris's. His tenure as either chairman or ranking minority member of the powerful Appropriations Committee was now nearly two decades long. Something was wrong. Harris's reporter's intuition was clanging in his head like a fire alarm.

"All I can tell you, Harris, is the staff said he's taking care of some family business. Now, if you'll excuse me, I'm late for a meeting." Boyer turned away. With a quick pace she headed toward the senators-only elevator, a sanctuary for members eager to escape the crowds and uncomfortable queries of journalists.

Harris followed right behind. He caught up to her near the elevator. He'd been part of these Kabuki dance questioning sessions long enough to know he could keep pestering his target until the elevator whisked them away. "So, you haven't talked to him. Is that correct? When was the last time you saw him or spoke to him?" *Crap! The door's already opening. I've lost her.*

Boyer's smile reflected in the mirror at the back of the elevator car as the doors closed behind her. The look in her eye said "I got you this time, Ward."

Harris switched off his recorder. The majority leader across the hallway was holding court facing a dozen microphones. Harris headed the opposite direction and down the stairs so that he could camp outside the main entrance to the Appropriations Committee offices. If the chairman wasn't there, at some point Pat Sistrunk would be. It was time to start squeezing his prey.

THIRTY-ONE

Yekaterinburg

Aaron hit the buzzer next to the door at the decrepit army institute building. He repeated the Russian phrase and the door buzzed open. The lights were on in Dr. Borisova's office and he walked through the open door, one arm behind his back.

Natasha looked up. He thought he detected a thin smile, a hint, perhaps, that his third appearance with vodka the previous night had begun to break down her barriers. From behind his back he pulled a bouquet of purple autumn crocus that he had spotted growing wild near his apartment building and handed them to her.

Her eyes widened and her mouth opened with a gasp. "They beautiful. Where you get?"

He smiled and shrugged. "I thought a little color might brighten your day in this gray weather."

She grabbed a coffee cup from her desk and filled it from the water cooler, then tucked the stems of the purple flowers in. She leaned her nose into the blossoms and smiled at the light honey nectar scent.

"I was hoping to find lilacs since I'm guessing they're your favorite, but it's not the right season."

"No find lilac here, now. But flower lovely. Thank you."

He approached her, hoping to be rewarded with a hug, but she turned away. His frustration was beginning to get the better of him. It was past time to eliminate the competition. "So, did you tell Kim you won't be needing him?"

Her smile was gone when she turned back to him. "Who say we not?"

"Well, it's just, okay, I assumed from our discussions that he wouldn't fit your needs. Was I wrong?"

"Not decided." Her tone was sharp.

Okay, I guess I've overreached. She's not ready to fill me in yet.

"Oh. I'm sorry, I thought—. No, forget I asked. Would today be a good day for me to be vaccinated?" He smiled again. "I get nervous being surrounded by the virus, especially since I'm the only one who hasn't been vaccinated. As I told you before, I am happy to infect the infidels, but I'm no martyr."

"I told *you* before, you cannot infect if vaccinated. If choose you do mission, you must have virus to infect others. Then get vaccine. Must remain unvaccinated or useless."

"I see. But maybe, then, you can tell me the details of how I will carry out our mission?"

"When time right, you learn. Now, please go, very busy."

Crap. This isn't working. The vodka and flowers haven't done the trick. He'd have to think of another way to get to her. He stood there for a second too long thinking of his next move.

Natasha looked over her shoulder and saw him still standing there. A smile crept onto her lips. "But thank you for flower. Very kind." The previous perfunctory tone was gone.

Aaron nodded, smiled, and turned to leave. *Okay, progress.*

THIRTY-TWO

The Capitol

Pat Sistrunk snuck out of the Appropriations Committee office through the side door and jumped on the elevator that his assistant had called. He'd been warned that the reporter Harris Ward was staked out at the front door of the office suite. Pat had been summoned to the majority leader's suite of offices on the second floor directly above the Appropriations Committee. He had no choice but to go.

Pat stood in the leader's reception area watching as four Democratic senators entered the leader's inner sanctum. Oregon's Elise Warnke, the leader's alter ego and policy director, had arrived first. She chatted briefly with the two admin assistants at their desks in the reception area before heading in. Pat smiled as she passed by. She seemed a little surprised to see him parked by the doorway to the inner sanctum.

Next was Rhode Island's Jonathon Rostow, the liaison with the press, who stomped past the staff and into the leader's private office, eyes straight ahead. Doug Haver of Maryland, the assistant majority leader, was third and he also ignored the staff and talked on his cell phone. Freshman senator Jimmy Capton from Illinois arrived fourth and, looking a little lost, actually knocked on the door before entering. Pat was well aware that the first two senators along with the leader were sometimes referred to as the troika, the Democratic brain trust. Haver was the whip, so it made sense he'd be included in most leadership meetings. But why was Capton there?

He didn't get much time to think about it as Leader Johnson strolled in accompanied by Larry Scholls, the secretary for the majority— Johnson's key staffer. The six-foot-tall, brown-haired majority leader, in a traditional dark suit and polished cowboy boots, was talking on his cell phone. He walked past Pat into his private office followed by Scholls. Pat didn't move. His hands were in his pockets so no one could see them shaking. Larry turned and motioned for Pat to join them.

"Are you sure?" Pat whispered.

"Get in here, Sistrunk," Larry growled.

"Okay. Say, Larry, can you tell me what this is about?" Pat smiled, trying to suppress his anxiety.

Larry stopped and turned around. "What do you think?"

Pat shrugged. "I've never been summoned to a meeting like this. Except with the chairman. And even then, I'm usually told to wait outside. Are you sure I'm supposed to be in there?"

Scholls shook his head and threw up his hands. "I assure you, you're supposed to be here. Now come on. We can't keep the senators waiting."

Pat followed Larry through the leadership suite and into the leader's office. His first thought was, *Gee, this is like my office right downstairs.* Sunlight was streaming in from the west. A view of the Washington Monument was framed by the nearly floor-to-ceiling windows. The leader was standing behind an enormous mahogany desk at the far end. The four other senators perched on Louis XIV furniture in the center of the room. Scholls closed the door and indicated Pat should stand against the wall next to him.

The leader came around his desk and took the largest chair. "What

I'm going to tell you cannot leave this room." He stared at the whip, Senator Haver. "And I mean no one. Got it, Doug?"

Scholls chuckled under his breath.

"Sure, Charley. Whatever you say," Haver replied, sounding like the lap dog he pretended to be in these meetings, the one who would surely bite you in the ass if you turned your back on him.

Pat caught Senator Warnke staring in his direction. Her piercing hazel-eyed gaze beneath a thick brown pageboy at least twenty years out of date sent a quick shiver down his spine. She turned back toward the leader and said, "Does this have something to do with Harry's absence? My staff says no one has seen him since August." She glanced back at Pat. He thought he might lose control of his bladder.

The leader smiled. "I should have known you'd figure it out. Yes. That's why I invited Pat Sistrunk to join us." He turned to the freshman, Capton, explaining, "Pat is Lackland's Appropriations staff director, Jimmy." He looked to the corner where Pat was trying to hide. "Pat, tell us what you know about Harry's absence."

The sweat start rolling from his hairline onto his shirt collar. He looked at Larry Scholls for help.

Scholls rolled his hand as if urging Pat to respond.

"Um, yes, sir, um, Mr. Leader, um, Senator. I'm not sure what I should say. Mrs. Lackland told me—"

"Damn it, Sistrunk. Tell them what you told me. Harry had a stroke. What more do you know?"

There was an audible gasp from Warnke and Rostow. Haver grabbed his head with both hands. The more junior senator, Capton, didn't react.

"Oh my God, Charley," Elise Warnke blinked back a tear, "is he okay?"

Charley Johnson shook his head. "C'mon, Pat, give us the details. I don't care what Beverly Lackland told you."

Pat sighed. "Yes, sir. Senators, about one week into the August recess Senator Lackland was found in his Capitol office by a maintenance man who summoned the Capitol physician. They determined he'd had a stroke. They rushed him to the hospital, but by the time they got there the damage was done. The doctors say he won't likely recover, although he's still alive."

"What does the press know?" Rostow piped up.

Pat shrugged. "Beverly, um, Mrs. Lackland, told me not to tell anyone. She says she's holding out hope he'll recover." His lip quivered a little and he cleared his throat while shaking his head. "But it's been nearly two months and," he shrugged again. His shoulders sagged, as if air was draining from his balloon.

The five senators sat motionless, staring at him, clearly awaiting a more complete answer to Rostow's question.

Pat continued. "As far as I know, the press is unaware. Although that *Roll Call* reporter, Harris Ward, keeps asking." Pat looked at each member. "He says he wants to interview the chairman. I keep putting him off, but I think it's only a matter of time before—"

"And that's why we're meeting," Charley interrupted. "Jon, how do we hold off the press?"

"We can't." The short, balding man with a round face and bushy eyebrows responded with New England frankness. "Not really. Well, maybe till after the election. This is our last week before we recess. Senators want to go home. The candidates need to campaign."

"Why don't we tell them the truth?" Senator Warnke asked. She cast a stern glance at each of them. "Tell them he's recovering from a stroke. We don't have to go into the details. In fact, Jon, we tell them that privacy laws forbid us from talking about the specifics. That way we get in front of the story before it gets out of control."

Senator Haver said, "Well, I think—"

Johnson cut him off. "What do you say, Jon?"

"I don't know." Jon Rostow edged forward in his seat, nearer to the leader. "If we say anything, the press will demand to know the details. When did it happen? What's his status? What hospital provided care? They'll eke out the rest. Nothing ever stays a secret in this town. I think you've got to keep the lid on as long as you can. Besides, like I said, it's only one more week. Once we're out of town, the issue will fade. And after the elections, it probably won't make any difference. Right, Jimmy?"

Senator Capton flinched as his name was spoken. "I'm not sure what you mean, Senator."

Charley Johnson spoke in a soothing tone. "Senator Capton, Jimmy, what Jon is asking is what is the latest prognosis for the elections. We're clinging to a one-vote majority now. If we lose Harry's seat in Virginia, well . . . You're the head of the campaign committee. Is that going to change come November?"

"Oh, I see." Capton sat up straighter. "As I told you last month, we still think we'll pick up three seats. Pennsylvania's a slam dunk; Hampton's up by twenty points. Miller is doing very well in Iowa, and it looks like Caine is going to win New Hampshire. All our incumbents are safe except Georgia. I guess if something were to happen to Senator Lackland—"

"It already has," Senator Warnke interjected.

Capton nodded. "Yes, well, even so, worst case, we'd certainly expect to keep the majority by a vote."

Johnson slapped his hands on the wooden arms of his chair and started to stand up, signaling the end of the meeting. "That's good enough for me. We keep this close until after the election. If you get cornered, Senator Rostow, just tell the press as far as you know Harry's been tending to some personal matters."

"But how do we know this is still a secret, Charley?" Elise Warnke hadn't moved. She tilted her head back and narrowed her eyes.

Charley Johnson sank back in his seat and studied her for a moment. He turned to Pat. "Pat, as far as you know, does anyone else besides Beverly and the doctors know what happened to Harry?"

Pat thought for a moment before responding. "Well, there is the guy from the fireplace crew who found him."

Johnson waved his hand in dismissal. "He wouldn't know what happened. Would he?"

Pat nodded and raised his eyes, as if beseeching heaven. "Well, um, Senator, um, the chairman did have a meeting with Senator Clayborn after the stroke."

"What?" Johnson jumped in his seat. "How did he have a meeting? I thought you told me he was almost catatonic."

"Yes, sir. Um, Beverly, Mrs. Lackland, did all the talking. Senator Lackland sat on the couch. He just stared into space." Pat blinked back tears. "After Mrs. Lackland ushered Senator Clayborn out, she told me no more meetings." He dropped his head. "That was the last time I saw the chairman."

"Jesus, Mary, and Joseph," Johnson gasped. "So, she has him meet with a Republican. What the hell was she thinking?"

"Well, I think it's obvious, Charley." Senator Warnke leaned in. "She didn't want to lose her position as *Mrs.* Senator Lackland." She smiled a hard smile. "After all, if something happens to the chairman, well, Harry's not a rich man and she's just Beverly Lackland, former Senate receptionist." She paused. "At least she was smart enough to realize he couldn't be seen in public. Too bad it was after she had that meeting." She paused again. "Are you still sure about the strategy, Charley?"

Johnson bristled and then smiled. "Elise, you're the smartest one in these meetings and that's why I count on you. But this time we don't have a choice. If the Republicans think they should be in the majority, you know they'll press the point. Plus they'll use that nugget to increase their fundraising calls. Right now, we see Republican donors walking away from Senate races. Right, Jimmy?"

Jimmy nodded.

"They can read the tea leaves," the leader continued. "But with Virginia gone, if we lose Georgia, we'd have to win all three contested states or we'd be out. We've got to keep this quiet."

"Well, how are you going to do that? Who's going to run the Appropriations Committee between now and the election?" Elise asked.

Charley Johnson looked up at Pat and smiled. "I think Pat can handle the committee for now. Can't you, Pat?"

Pat's mouth dropped open and he blinked furiously.

Larry Scholls put his hand over his mouth and leaned toward Pat. "Just shut your pie hole and nod," he whispered.

Pat closed his mouth and nodded.

THIRTY-THREE

Southern Maryland

"Hey, Fred, it's Paula. Got a minute?"

Fred Hendricks leaned back in his Adirondack chair and smiled. A passing cloud momentarily blocked the sun and a breeze had come up. The Patuxent River running by his cabin in southern Maryland was showing some ripples. He shivered and wished he'd grabbed a jacket before coming out to enjoy some fall sunshine and humidity-free air. "Paula," he laughed, "I got all the time in the world. But this is a surprise. Twice in one month. What can I do for you?"

"Oh, it's that same thing we talked about. Did you see the news about a massacre in Kazakhstan?"

"Yeah, awful. You think that's what the rumors are about?"

"It's gotta be. I'm worried that our government is looking at the wrong suspect and not doing anything to stop the virus from getting loose."

"Jesus, that's terrible. What's your boss think?"

"Oh man, Fred. I haven't even told Senator Boyer. She's pretty tough, you know, and I haven't had much time to develop a relationship."

"I get it. What else can you do, though?"

"I told Pat. But that was useless."

"Hah, what'd you expect?"

"Jeepers, Fred. He's the committee staff director. You'd think he'd have something to offer."

"Paula, have you forgotten how he got the job?"

"What do you mean?"

"Pat Sistrunk was Chairman Lackland's driver. He'd started out in the mail room and volunteered to drive the chairman when the old man was getting up there in years. Pat always knew a lot of jokes and he kept the boss entertained as he chauffeured him around town. They got pretty close."

"Well, how'd he go from comedic driver to staff director?"

"That's a metaphor for how the Hill works. This is what he told me one night a dozen or so years ago before he quit drinking. I probably shouldn't repeat it, but given the circumstances, what the hell.

"One morning on the drive to the Capitol, Lackland was complaining that his accountant had retired and he had no one to do his taxes. Pat told him that he could get Lackland's taxes done for free. He promised he'd keep the information private. Lackland was wary, but he's also incredibly cheap. The part about it being free sounded real good. So, he agreed to let Pat try.

"Well, Pat told me he was able to get Lackland a big refund, and the chairman was thrilled. For the next couple years, Pat took care of his taxes. Then when the Treasury-Postal clerk quit—that's the old name of the Financial Services Subcommittee. They used to handle the IRS. Anyway, when that guy quit Lackland gave Pat the job. So, to keep a long story short . . ."

Paula smiled. *Now that's the Fred Hendricks I remember. His idea of a short story is* War and Peace. *But like he said, he's got all the time in the world. . . . It is interesting.*

"Pat had a sharp assistant on Treasury and she kept him out of trouble. Eventually, Lackland made him committee staff director. I'll give Pat credit for one thing, though. He was always smart enough to surround himself with good staff."

"He must have something going for him if he could do the chairman's taxes and get him a big refund."

"Hah. Now that's the kicker. What Pat never told the chairman was his wife's sister was a tax accountant. Pat would do some handyman things around his sister-in-law's house and she did the boss's taxes for free. Now, ain't that something?"

"Oh Lord, so the chairman's AWOL. We have a clueless staff director running the Appropriations Committee. A bunch of terrorists are about to unleash a deadly biological weapon that could destroy us all, and the White House is in denial."

"That's about the sound of it. Hey, Paula, welcome back."

THIRTY-FOUR

White House

Steve Simpson stood in front of the Resolute Desk waiting for President Parker to hang up the phone. He glanced at his cell phone and looked up as the president ended his call. "Mr. President, looks like all's on track for the G-7 meeting. The leaders—"

"Have they broken ground on the golf course?"

"Well, the good news is the Secret Service is backing your recommendation to clear-cut part of the forest, which paves the way for the golf course."

"When are they going to start? At this rate, I'll be retired before you get it built. Christ, Steve, what's taking so long?"

Steve sucked in a deep breath and paused. He wanted to get this right. "Mr. President, you're about to meet with the leaders of the free world. The Russ—. Someone is threatening us with a new and deadly coronavirus. I'd say the golf course should be the least of your worries."

Parker bristled. "Who are you to tell me what I should worry about? Anyway, it's not some terrorist outfit. It's the Chinese, Steve. Where are we in our plans to retake Hong Kong? We've got to teach them a lesson."

Steve lowered his head and snorted softly. Looking up, he spoke in a firm, clear voice. "Mr. President, with all due respect, we don't know who is behind the virus."

"Of course we do!" Parker bellowed, his nostrils flaring and face reddening.

Steve held up a hand. "Please, sir, let me finish."

Parker leaned back in his chair, but his eyes were tiny slits above his sneer even though his cheeks were a tad less crimson.

Steve absentmindedly checked his cell phone again, a common affliction, and then spoke. "Sir, our allies believe the Russians are behind this. The attack was right across the border with Russia. The threat is clearly aimed at the US, and they could very well be planning to attack the G-7 meeting. Putin is still livid he was kicked out of the old G-8." He took a quick breath.

"Our military says any act, if you will, to liberate Hong Kong will be met with extreme resistance from mainland China. They see no possible scenario in which we could accomplish this objective without enormous loss of life and an almost certain widening of the conflict, perhaps to include nuclear weapons. Further, there is scant evidence to believe the residents of Hong Kong want us to liberate them. And none of our Asian allies would support a unilateral attack. We simply cannot do so."

"But if China attacks us, we have to do something."

"Yes, sir, assuming all our intelligence is inaccurate and the Chinese are indeed behind an effort to attack the G-7, we'd have to retaliate. That's why the Joint Chiefs are war planning a blockade in the South China Sea to force Chinese forces to evacuate the artificial islands they've been building."

"Gee, that's real bold, Steve. Is that all those cowards want to do?"

"Quite candidly, sir, I think even that is fraught with risk. Our supply lines will be thousands of miles long, whereas the Chinese are right there. Even if we find that China is involved in this coronavirus, I'd urge you to think long and hard about this course of action. No one wants to start a conflict we can't control. Sir."

"All right. Just get those trees cut down and get my course started."

Steve perked up as another thought came to him. "Mr. President, a thought on that subject. With the operation in the Pacific, we have a real good reason to request that emergency supplemental now. That's the one to enhance security for the continuity of government, as we discussed." He smiled. "And cover for the golf course."

The president looked as if he understood and beamed.

Steve felt the buzz of his cell and scrolled to a message. "Uh, sir, there's a new message coming in from this Anti-Imperialist Society group. It's says we have one week to begin to pull back our troops.

"It says, quote, 'The imperialist Yankees have long held to their Monroe Doctrine which stipulates that foreign troops may not occupy nations in the Western Hemisphere. Yet they insist on occupying our nations and those of our neighbors in Asia, the Middle East, Africa, and Europe. These duplicitous policies are only the tip of the iceberg. It is time for the world to wake up. Their goal is the subjugation and outright control of all peoples. Our countries have long suffered the indignities of their illegal occupation. The time has come to end their imperial quest. We demand the removal of all US military forces stationed overseas and the disbandment of NATO immediately.

"'We will use any force at our disposal to eradicate this threat, even if it requires the elimination of the United States.

"'Mr. President, you have one week to act, or suffer irreversible consequences.

"'Signed,

"'The Liberation of South Korea Caucus

"'The Freedom for Eastern Europe Group

"'The Anti-Imperialist Society of the Arabian Peninsula and Djibouti

"'The Okinawa Independence movement.'"

Steve looked up from his phone. "Well, I guess we know they're serious. Mr. President, I think it's high time we started formulating a plan to root out this bioweapon at its source, no matter where that is."

"It's China, Steve. Start the blockade."

"First, sir, I'm going to tell OMB director O'Keefe to send an open-ended supplemental appropriations request to the Hill in response to the emergent threat."

"Fine. Then the blockade, Simpson."

THIRTY-FIVE

The Capitol

Percy Quenton strutted into Pat Sistrunk's office as his escort, Pat's assistant Gracie Shelten, slid out of his way. Quenton was the head of legislative affairs for the Office of Management and Budget. He'd previously worked for the House Republican leader before accepting the position at OMB in the second Parker term, probably hoping that it would lead to a job on the White House staff. But after nearly two years, he still had to grovel to Democratic staffers in the House and Senate. It was obvious to Pat that Quenton hated sucking up to the staff. He thought he was too important to be taken lightly.

Pat looked up at his mirror image, albeit thirty years younger, standing before his desk. "Yeah, Percy, what can I do you for? Heh." Pat detected a twinge from the executive branch representative at his fractured syntax but didn't care.

"Director O'Keefe wants to talk to the chairman." Percy leaned closer and dropped his voice a little. "It's supposed to come from him, so don't get me in trouble on this, but I thought you ought to know." He offered a conspiratorial smile. "He's calling to request an emergency national security supplemental because of this new coronavirus from the terrorist group. The president wants thirty billion ASAP in an emergency response fund like the one after 9/11 to enhance security and to cover DoD's response."

The thought of a new coronavirus made the hair on the back of Pat's neck stand up, but the notion of a phone call to the chairman brought on a wave of terror. "He can't call the chairman. He's too busy," Pat snapped.

"Too busy? Chairman Lackland's too busy to talk to a member of the president's cabinet?" Pat's blow-off seemed to set Quenton off. "I told you Director O'Keefe wants to request an emergency national security supplemental from the Appropriations Committee chairman. What part don't you understand?" Percy's tone was sharp, as if he had lost patience with Hill staff who failed to respect him.

Pat felt the fire coming from the White House flunky but stood firm, knowing he had no choice. "If it's national security, call Boyer. She's chairman of the Defense Subcommittee. She can handle this." He waved a dismissal.

Quenton didn't move, but Pat could see the trembling lips, the rapid breathing. "You're gonna regret this, Sistrunk. You can't fuck with us like this. Mark my words, asshole, you're going to be sorry."

Pat jumped up and leaned menacingly over his desk. "Who the heck do you think you are, Percy? You have no right to talk to me like that. You're just staff. Now get out."

"Well, who the hell do you think *you* are?" Quenton turned and stormed out.

Pat sat back down, calmed his agitated breathing, and drafted an email to Paula to warn Boyer that OMB might be calling to request a DoD supplemental. He was rereading this memo before hitting send when his cell phone rang. He didn't recognize the number.

"Hello?"

"Goddamn it, Sistrunk, who the hell do you think you are throwing my representative out of your office? You're not a senator!" Steve Simpson shouted over the phone. "Nobody elected you, pal!"

"Is that you, Simpson? Who do you think *you* are? I didn't throw that little jerk out, but I got work to do. He said his piece, I told him what to do, he just didn't like the idea."

"But you can't reject a call from the president's cabinet officer."

"Listen, I told him the chairman's too busy. He said it's for national security. He should call Chairman Boyer. She chairs the Defense Subcommittee. We don't need to bother Chairman Lackland with this." Like many others in the Senate, Lackland couldn't stand the former senator who was now president. But he acknowledged that the people had elected him and did his best to respect the office.

"Since when is the Appropriations Committee chairman too busy to take a call from the OMB director? It's his fucking job to take that call!"

Pat rolled his eyes and took a deep breath. "Look, Steve, Chairman Lackland is tied up with some family matters. The CR is done. We're shutting this place down. The Senate isn't going to entertain a sup until after the election. If O'Keefe wants to send up something now, it won't do any good. If he insists on talking about it, then he can talk to Boyer. She's the one he has to convince anyway. But I told you, the leader's sending the boys and girls home. Nobody's doing a sup now. You'll be lucky to get one in lame duck."

"But it's an emergency, Sistrunk. Don't you get that? We're about to get hit with another coronavirus. And it's ten times worse than COVID-19."

Hearing the word *COVID* again made Pat shiver. Thoughts of Edwina filled his head. He regained his composure. "Emergency or not, you're going to have to deal with it without talking to the chairman."

"Oh yeah, is he too busy to talk to the president? Is he going to refuse that call?"

Oh boy. The president. That would be a problem.

Pat racked his brain and spoke in a very calm voice to defuse the tension. He had to eliminate any chance that the president would try to call Lackland. "Steve, old friend," he had a hard time getting those words out since he and Simpson had never been friends. Steve Simpson and President Parker, then a senator, had spent years trying to gut the authority of the Appropriations Committee. "The majority leader told me personally that we're done. We're going home. Our candidates aren't going to be trapped in DC a couple weeks before the election. If the president really wants to weigh in on this, I suggest he call the leader, Charley Johnson. And if your OMB director needs to talk to someone, tell him to call Boyer. That's the best advice I can give you. It's nothing personal, Steve. Like you, I got a job to do." Pat crossed his fingers hoping that sounded genuine. There was a long silence.

Finally, Simpson spoke. "Goddamn it, Pat. I'm not going to forget this. But I understand what you're saying. You got a pair of brass balls on you. You better hope they don't get caught in a vise." The phone slammed down.

Pat leaned back. *Holy mother of God, I hope that worked.*

THIRTY-SIX

Dirksen Senate Office Building

"This is Paula," she said in a quizzical tone after looking at the unrecognized number on her cell phone.

"Paula, it's Chauncey. I need—"

"Hey, honey, can I call you back? I'm right in the middle of a staff meeting."

"NO!" His voice sounded panicky. "Paula, don't hang up." She heard a deep sigh. "I'm at the police station in Dumfries, Virginia. I've been arrested. I need your help. They think I was kidnapping Charlie and Ross! They told me I could call a lawyer, but I called you. You've got to come out here and explain to them I'm their father, not a kidnapper."

Paula half stood. "Wha? What are you talking about?"

"Some white woman, some Karen, saw me trying to put Charlie in his bike seat. He was throwing a tantrum because he wanted to ride on the old-fashioned mechanical horse at the shopping mall. The lady started screaming for the police. She was shrieking, saying I was trying to kidnap the boys. Charlie started yelling that he wanted his mama. So Ross started to cry, too."

"Oh, my God, Chauncey, are the boys okay?"

"They've taken them. I don't know where they are! They were pretty shook up. You've got to come here and straighten this out."

With one hand, Paula tapped the stack of documents on her lap into order and shoved them onto the couch beside her. "But why did they arrest you?"

"I started yelling at the white woman to shut up, because she was scaring the boys. About that time a police car drove up and without any chance to explain, they told *me* to shut up, handcuffed me, and put me in the back of the squad car. We waited there until another cop arrived, who took the boys. They brought me here. But, please, can you just come. I can explain everything later."

"Oh, my goodness, yes of course! Wait. Where are you?"

"The police station. I don't know the address. It's in Dumfries, Virginia."

"Okay, I'll find it. Please stay calm. We'll get this worked out. I'm so sorry, Chaunce."

"Lot of good that does," he snapped. "Just come. Now!"

Paula punched off her cell phone, glanced around the room, stood up, and grabbed her purse. Her staff was staring at her, a few mouths wide open.

She stopped for a second. "Okay, um, Chauncey's been arrested. It's a case of mistaken identity. They thought he was kidnapping our boys. I've got to go. I'll be back as soon as I can."

She scanned the room and focused first on Stevie Guy and then on her clerical assistant, Larraine. "Can we please keep this quiet? I'm sure it's all a mistake. Larraine, if the chairman or full committee calls for me, pass them on to Stevie. Stevie, I'll leave it to your discretion what you tell them. Let them know I'll be back as soon as I can. Anyone else, Larraine, take a message. Please, everyone, please keep this between us.

I got to go. Um, we'll reconvene when I get back. But don't hang around tonight if I'm not back by then. Okay." She rushed from the room and quick-walked to the exit.

THIRTY-SEVEN

The Capitol

"What do you mean I can't go back there? Don't you know who I am? I need to talk to Harry." Senator Boyer was standing in S-128, the anteroom of the Appropriations Committee suite of offices. Her nostrils flared and her arms were crossed, but not one dark hair on her sleek head was out of place in her bluster.

Gracie Shelten stood in front of the attractive junior senator from California attempting a road block. She looked as nervous as a robin facing a hungry cat poised to pounce. "The chairman, er, ah, isn't available, um, Senator Boyer." Pat Sistrunk's secretary stumbled over the words.

"That's what everyone keeps saying. Then I'll talk to Pat." Boyer extended her arm and pushed past the administrative aide. She stormed through the outer office and into Pat's space. "Where's Harry, Pat?" She glared at him.

Pat stood up and walked around to the front of his desk. To his right sat the chairman's small private office. Its lights were turned off. Boyer glanced at the darkened room and looked back at Pat.

"This is ridiculous, Pat. Where is he?"

"Senator Boyer," Pat spoke in a soothing voice, "the chairman is attending to family matters in Virginia. His wife has asked that he not be bothered and we are accommodating his and her wishes. What seems to be the problem?"

"I just got off the phone with Defense Secretary Vest. He says the president is requesting an emergency supplemental to deal with anticipated costs of this new virus that the terrorists are threatening us with. He told me Harry wouldn't take the president's call. Is that true? Harry wouldn't talk to President Parker?"

Pat smirked and shook his head. "I can assure you, Senator, the chairman did no such thing. I heard from Steve Simpson, who works for Parker. I told him that since the matter was national security his staff from OMB would be well served talking to you. After all, you're the Defense Subcommittee chairman. It's your responsibility. I can categorically deny that the chairman refused a call from the president. Never happened."

Boyer appeared to relax a little. "Well, why wasn't I warned about this in advance? That gal you hired to work for me," an accusatory finger aimed at Pat, "is nowhere to be found."

"What? That doesn't sound like Paula. She's solid as they come."

"Well, solid like a rock or not, she's what the military call AWOL. Her secretary gave me the same BS. Something about a family commitment. There seems to be a lot of that going around." Boyer scoffed and continued, "So, what are we going to do about the secretary's message?"

Pat scrunched up his face. "Paula's secretary?"

"No, Pat. Secretary Vest. He wants something like thirty billion dollars with no strings attached."

The smirk reappeared on Pat's face. "I told them there was no chance until after the election and that they need to submit their request to the committee formally." He puffed himself up. "Harry

Lackland doesn't work for this or any other president. The United States Senate is a separate branch of government. The chairman won't be treated like a flunky. They need to prepare a real budget request. Then the committee, and your subcommittee in particular, Senator Boyer, can determine what funds should be appropriated. And that won't happen until after the election, no matter what President Parker or Steve Simpson wants."

His sharp tone startled Boyer, but she seemed to approve of the sentiment. "Alright then, we'll wait till we get a request." She wagged a finger at him. "But you better find that gal and get her back to work." The index finger was pointing at him again. "I don't appreciate being given the run-around." Her irritability was front and center. "Not from her or from you either, Pat. When you talk to Harry, tell him I want to talk to him. He needs to get back here. There's a lot of whispering going on." She spun and left.

THIRTY-EIGHT

Yekaterinburg

"Get in here, now." Dr. Borisova's face was pale, nearly as gray as the autumnal Russian weather.

Aaron cautiously entered her apartment. Clearly, something was wrong. He instinctively reached into his jacket pocket and grasped his switchblade. "What's wrong?" He tried to mask his anxiety and sound an empathetic tone.

Natasha Borisova was pacing back and forth in the tiny apartment, smoking. He'd never seen her smoke before. His hand relaxed and he reached out to offer a hug.

She waved him away. "What wrong with you? How you not see?"

He raised his palms in surrender. "See what?"

"Kim disappear."

Aaron had to suppress his smile. *That's good news. You have no choice but to use me after all.* "What? That's terrible. Did something happen to him? Do you suppose the Americans captured him?"

"We not know. Apartment empty. No sign struggle. We believe he fled." She released a large sigh. "As you said, I told him because of changes, we cannot use him."

Aaron tried to appear puzzled. "But what's the problem, then? If you don't need him, so what if he left? He probably went home. Why stay around?" He guffawed. "It couldn't be for the weather. Although, from what I understand, Pyongyang isn't much nicer this time of year." He smiled, trying to ease her obvious tension.

"Is not funny. What you not understand. He took virus. And maybe vaccine. We not know Korean government plan." She took an especially long drag on the cigarette, placed the butt under the kitchen faucet, and tossed the soggy smoke into the trash.

Aaron saw a bottle of vodka on the kitchen counter and circled behind Natasha, opened a cabinet, and removed two glasses. He poured two double shots and handed her one. "Here, I think you need this." He threw back the shot.

Natasha glared at him but poured the vodka down her throat and replaced the glass on the counter.

He poured another round, filling the short glasses to the rim. He handed her one, clinked it, and drank.

She paused.

"Go ahead," he said. "It will help you calm down. Besides, Kim is our ally. Whatever his government plans to do with the virus, it will surely be in our interest."

She shook her head. Tears welling in her eyes. "You not understand." She downed the vodka but held onto her glass. "I not want virus release. I only want imperialistic Americans and your enemy, Jews," she nodded in his direction, "stop aggression. Leave Russia alone. And you Arab people deserve peace. But each year more American soldiers on borders, and weapons. They say deterrent. We know better. Troops, missiles weaken Russia and military. Someday, maybe soon, they blackmail. Demand we return Crimea to Ukraine even though Russian live there. Remove friends from Belarus, Moldova, and Eastern Ukraine. They want surround and then . . ." She waved the empty glass and a tear spilled onto her cheek.

She continued, "We see Western power when not stopped. Russians never forget German in St. Petersburg or French in Moscow. Now American threaten with NATO." She placed the glass on the counter and signaled for him to pour.

I guess our intelligence was right. She is sympathetic. But now it's out of her control. "But Kim could ruin your plans," he noted solemnly.

"Yes. Terrible for world."

He reached out to hug her again. This time she moved closer. She started to tremble and then released anguished sobs in his arms. Aaron held her close and stroked her hair. He whispered, "Please don't cry. Who knows? It's only the North Koreans. They tend to screw up everything they try. Think of all those missiles that explode as soon as they take off. It could be worse."

She pulled back. "How worse?"

"It could have been me who stole the virus. Our success rate is much higher." He smiled.

She jerked upright, then relaxed and chuckled.

He turned her head and, cupping her chin gently, he kissed her.

THIRTY-NINE

ROLL CALL

WHERE'S HARRY?
By Harris Ward, Washington, DC

It's been more than two months since Virginia senator Harry Lackland, the powerful chairman of the Senate's Appropriations Committee, has been seen in the Capitol. The long-serving and crafty politician, with a reputation for ruling with an iron fist, has failed to vote since the Senate returned from the August recess. Even more surprising, he failed to attend his committee's markup of the stopgap spending bill or to manage its consideration on the Senate floor. Neither his office nor Democratic leadership is offering much explanation for the octogenarian's unprecedented absence.

According to an unnamed aide, the senator has been attending to family matters in recent weeks. Although senators occasionally miss routine votes and sometimes allow pressing family commitments to take precedence over fulfilling their constitutional duties to be in attendance and vote on all matters, this is the first time in *Roll Call*'s knowledge that an absence of such length has gone virtually unexplained by the member, his or her office, and the party.

At *Roll Call*, we do not speculate on the health of members of

Congress. But without any explanation, several unnamed members have questioned the chairman's absence. As one unnamed senator whispered, "We're all beginning to wonder, 'Where's Harry?'"

"Goddamn it!" Majority leader Charley Johnson finished scrolling through the article, clicked off his cell phone, and bounced it off the stacks of paper on his desktop. "Who the hell is talking to the press? Jesus H. Christ. We're weeks out from the election and this crap has to get out. God, I hope it's too late for the bastards to turn their fundraising back on." He looked up at Rhode Island's Senator Rostow, the de facto press guru for the Democrats who was standing in front of the desk. "What do we do now?"

Rostow gave a one-shoulder shrug. "I think the best strategy is kick it to Beverly Lackland. We can start a whisper campaign that she's holding back the details. We'll add that, from what little she has told us, Lackland is recovering from an illness and will be back in the Capitol after the election."

"That's what Elise wanted to do last week. I swear to God, Jon. She's almost always right. But isn't it too late for that? I mean, the genie's out of the bottle."

"Well, yes and no, Leader. All the press seems to know is that Harry's not here. They don't know he's, um, incapacitated. Like Elise suggested, we tell them half the story. And keep our fingers crossed that the rest doesn't leak until after Election Day."

Charley Johnson rubbed his stubbled chin and said, "Yeah, okay, that's probably the best we can do. Find someone to leak this half of the story. That goddamned Ward, I swear he knows more about what's going on around here than I do. And I'm the one who's supposed to be running the place."

FORTY

Dirksen Senate Office Building

"Paula?" Stevie Guy opened the heavy metal door and knocked on the doorjamb between the staff office suite and her space. "Is everything okay? I mean with Chauncey."

Paula looked up from her desk. Her eyes were red and the smile that always graced her face was absent. "Oh, Stevie, yeah, I guess, considering . . . Chauncey's out of jail." She shrugged with the resignation of one who has survived a trauma, but not quite unscathed. "The police even kinda apologized for the mistake. It took me showing them the boys' birth certificates and a family picture to get them to understand. But it's not something either one of us are going to forget easily. Chauncey's furious. He wants to move back home—Hawaii, I mean. He says this is no place for our family. That people are always going to treat us differently here. And I hate to say it, but he's probably right. And the fact that his skin is so much darker than the boys', and Charlie's hair is almost blond, well, you know. Anyway, I don't know. And with all this new COVID threat stuff going on, I mean, it's . . ."

At the other doorway, Larraine Walker peeked in and said, "Paula, there's a General Gianini on your line. Says it's urgent. He needs to speak to you on a secure phone."

Stevie Guy waved goodbye and shut the door.

"Oh boy, okay, thanks, Larraine. Give me thirty seconds and transfer him to the vault." Paula stood up and rushed to the secure facility. When the phone rang, she picked it up noting that it was secure. "Al? What's up?"

"Paula, I thought you should know, the scuttlebutt is we're about to set up a blockade around one of those artificial islands that the Chinese constructed in the Spratly archipelago in the South China Sea, the area that the Philippines and almost everyone else claim are their territorial waters."

"Oh no. You can't be serious. The doggone White House must still be on this anti-China kick."

"That's right. I think it has to do with the latest ultimatum that the terrorists released. I'm sure you've seen it, right?"

"Actually, I haven't. I had a little, um, personal emergency to work out. What did they say?"

"They announced we've got one week to start bringing our troops home, or they'll release the virus. They're threatening to eliminate the United States."

"So, we're retaliating by threatening China? This is crazy. What are we going to do?"

"I talked to the CINC—well, 'Commander' they call him now— Admiral Cooper. He seems like a good guy. He understands what I told him, but of course he's got to follow orders. He did offer to help in any way if there's something he can do."

"Well, that's good. I guess I'm going to have to talk to my boss and explain all this. Now that we're getting ready to blockade China. I can use that excuse to tell her most of what I know. She's a smart woman, maybe she'll have an idea. And, if nothing else, she's a senator. She's got a loud voice. People listen when senators talk. Unlike the rest of us, I mean."

"Yeah, perhaps. Not sure what any of us mere mortals can do. You mentioned a personal emergency. Is everything okay?"

"Yes, now it is. Thanks. Just a misunderstanding. All good." Her lower lip trembled as she spoke and she willed back a tear.

The electronic buzz announced that the door was opening. Larraine's face appeared. Paula quickly wiped her eyes. "Just a second, Al." She covered the mouthpiece and spoke softly, "What is it, Larraine?"

"I'm sorry, Paula, but there's another gentleman who insists it's urgent that he speak to you immediately. He said his name is Ari Schweitzman."

Paula closed her eyes and threw back her head. She raised an index finger in Larraine's direction. "Hey, Al, I got to run. But can you give me Admiral Cooper's number just in case? If I think of anything else, I'll be in touch." She clicked off. "Okay, Larraine, put him through."

Paula, picking up the ringing phone, turned off its secure feature. "Hello, Mr. Schweitzman?"

"Yes, thank you for taking my call, Paula. And, please, call me Ari. This matter is extremely urgent. We have reason to believe that the new coronavirus has been released from the laboratory where they manufacture it."

"Oh dear. But I was told they gave us a week to respond."

"Yes, I heard the same thing. Unfortunately, a vial of the virus was stolen by a North Korean agent. And, apparently, neither our people nor those who manufactured the virus know what he intends to do with it. But we know it can't be good. Even one vial could destroy all of mankind. My country is working on a plan to obtain the vaccine, but I fear by the time we get it, it could be too late. Please let your government know, this might be the last chance to save the world. They must help us."

"Tell me how we can help and I'll pass the message on. I'm just not sure anyone will listen."

FORTY-ONE

2:00 a.m.
Yekaterinburg

The go-ahead had come from Aaron's local contact. The plan seemed simple enough—too simple. But there was no going back. The North Koreans had the virus. He couldn't wait any longer.

As instructed, Aaron had chained and locked the Army Artillery Institute's rusty gate and positioned a motorcycle at the edge of the forest across from the twelve-foot cyclone fence on the south side of the facility. Now there was just the matter of sprinting across the ten-foot buffer zone, hopping the fence, breaking into the building, and stealing the heavily guarded vaccine and a vial or two of the virus for American scientists to study—all before anyone came to stop him. Oh yeah, and a two-hundred-kilometer ride to the Kazakhstan border. And then, just maybe, a handoff to someone who could get the vaccine to the US. Easy peasy.

Shivering in the frosty night air, he pulled the black knit ski mask a little lower so that only his dark eyes and bushy beard were visible. Lock picks in his right jacket pocket, check. Switchblade in his left, and a 9mm pistol taped to his back, check and check. All good. Deep breath. Move out.

He hit the fence with his studded boot at forty inches off the ground, thrust his body upward, grabbed the top of the barrier with both gloved hands right below the concertina barbed wire, and flipped over like a pole vaulter. He landed hard on his back and lay flat on the ground, trying to catch his breath, half expecting sirens, lights, and guard dogs. . . . Nothing.

He rolled over, got to a crouch, and then launched himself across the unkempt space up to the building. So far so good. He eased over to a large window and peered inside. All dark. All good. The window's lock was a simple mechanism. He reached under his jacket and shirt and removed one piece of tape from his back while making sure his pistol was still secure. He pressed the tape onto the window. Using the butt end of his knife, he tapped on the glass, breaking enough to allow him to reach inside and unlock the window. No alarm. Could it really be that they felt hiding in plain sight was enough defense for the building? The hair on the back of his neck stood up. That didn't seem like the Russians. But no time to worry.

He jimmied his knife blade under the window and lifted it. Still nothing. He looked at the open window frame for the telltale signs of a silent alarm. No wires, no unusual padding in the corners that might send an electronic signal when opened. *This is too easy.*

The door to Borisova's ground-floor office was unlocked. He moved in the dark to the doorway to the stairs leading down to the basement lab. Again, unlocked. *It's got to be a trap, but I've got no choice. The Korean has the virus. He might have already unleashed it. Our only hope is to get the vaccine and reverse engineer it before it's too late.*

At the bottom of the stairs, he reached for the doorknob to the lab entrance. Locked. *Hmm. At least there's some defense. But still fishy.* He rechecked his knife and pistol and grabbed his lock picks. He'd studied the lock on previous visits. It seemed simple enough. With a few twists of the picks, he heard the soft click of the mechanism releasing.

Slowly, he turned the knob and pushed the door open a crack. A quiet hum from the refrigeration unit. Its bright blue display offered enough light to see. He pushed the door open wide enough to walk in, one pocketed hand on his knife. He turned to the vaccine storage room. That door was locked too. He pulled out the lock picks again and snapped the lock open in seconds.

He dared not turn on an additional light and fumbled around in the dimly lit room. He opened a box and found a syringe and eight vials of the vaccine. He stripped off his mask, jacket, heavy sweater, and long-sleeved T-shirt. He jabbed his arm.

He reached for the box of vaccine and was momentarily blinded when bright lights illuminated the vaccine room.

"So, this how you repay trust?" Dr. Borisova stood in the doorway to the stairs wearing a heavy coat and fur hat, aiming a pistol at Aaron. "Let me guess, you worry for safety. Decide break in and vaccinate." She smirked.

Aaron's eyes had adjusted and he held up his hands in surrender. "You got me. I'm sorry, but as I told you, I was uncomfortable being here every day with the virus so close. Especially now that Kim is out there somewhere." He waved at the room where the virus was stored.

She appraised him steadily but did not say anything.

"And you never let me know the plan—how I would expose the others while staying safe. I told you I'm no martyr. You must understand. I mean no harm, really." He shrugged, started to lower his hands, and took a step toward her. A smile spread across his face.

She side-stepped into the lab, saying, "Keep hands up. Don't come close. I know you trained killer." She turned her back to the still-dark hallway opposite the stairs, keeping the gun trained on Aaron. She motioned with the pistol for him to leave the vaccine area toward the stairway. "Now back up stair."

With his hands raised and facing her, he pleaded the whole way, "Please, Natasha, let me grab my jacket. I'll freeze to death."

"Hah. You won't live enough. Do what I say. Move slowly, out door."

"Please, Natasha, you've got this all wrong. We're partners. You need me to carry out your plan."

"Plan change. Virus already released. No threaten G-7 meeting. Must take credit when Korea attack. And hope works. You loose end. I did not want to kill before, but you betray. So, now you die. Move."

Aaron had to act immediately. She didn't know he had a pistol. He'd have to drop to the floor, grab his gun, and shoot, hoping she'd miss her first shot. He took a deep breath and paused. He didn't want to kill her, but what choice was she giving him? Something moved in the dark behind the doctor. Guards?

The shadow shot forward. Aaron dove onto the floor, rolled, and brought his gun up as a loud crash erupted. Natasha fell unconscious to the ground. Aaron trained his gun on the old Jewish cleaning woman. She was still holding the metal garbage can she had swung and connected with the back of Natasha's head.

"Don't shoot, Aaron," she rasped in English. "Quickly, get the vaccine and go. A bomb will explode in four minutes."

"What? Who are you? You can't destroy the vaccine and the virus with a bomb. What if the explosion causes it to spread?"

"The plan has changed. Headquarters decided. You are to get the vaccine and leave. This facility must be destroyed completely."

"What about the virus?"

"It will be destroyed. You must get to the Americans."

"But how? A two-hundred-kilometer race to the border? They'll stop me for sure now."

"Our agent, the bald man, will take you. Meet him on the other side of the woods. Now go."

"What about her?" He pushed his chin toward Natasha's inert form.

"The shiksa will meet the fiery death she deserves."

"No. I won't let you kill her." Aaron stood up, stuck his gun into his back waistband, and threw on his shirt, sweater, and jacket, keeping his eyes locked on the old woman's. He grabbed a half dozen vaccine vials and slid them carefully into his jacket pocket with the lock picks. He zipped it up.

"She must die. She is a killer. She is anti-Semite. She deserves to die."

"No. I will not be responsible for the death of another woman." His right hand snaked under his sweater and shirt and he brought out his gun and trained it on the old woman. "Unless you want to die?"

"You can't spare her. She will kill you the first chance she gets."

"Look, she's going to be out for a while. I'm putting her in one of the abandoned cars in the parking lot, far enough away and out of the cold. Don't you even think of neutralizing her." With exaggerated motion, he slid his finger onto the trigger.

The old woman sneered. "Take the bitch, then. But you're a fool. Now go. There isn't much time."

Aaron scooped up Natasha's limp body and threw her over his shoulder. He rushed up the stairs, kicked open the door to outside, and hustled over to a rusty sedan slumped against the rotting curb. He pushed her unconscious body into the passenger seat.

"Please don't try to re-create the virus, and remember we have the vaccine." He slapped a kiss on her forehead, slammed the door shut, vaulted back over the fence, and ran for his stashed motorcycle. The engine had cooled and it took a few tries to fire it up, but then he slammed it in gear and shot off through the woods.

A loud blast shattered the frosty night. He glanced behind him and a ball of fire soared up into the inky sky. He turned forward and hit the accelerator.

FORTY-TWO

Arlington, Virginia

Beverly Lackland stood on the front stoop of her brick colonial home. The entrance was framed by two white Corinthian columns and square-cut boxwoods. She looked out on the gaggle of reporters, television cameras, and microphones positioned on the sidewalk, some fifteen feet away across the narrow expanse of thick green lawn.

Her dark hair was tightly coiffed. She wore a bright floral-patterned wrap dress that showed off her bronzed tanning-salon legs and pink stiletto heels. Shivering in the late October sunshine, she glanced down a few times at a notecard she grasped with both hands. "Uh-hh-hh, hmm." She cleared her throat and in a timid voice, just above a whisper, addressed the press.

"Speak up, Mrs. Lackland!" a voice shouted.

She cleared her throat again, glaring across the yard, and spoke in a louder voice akin to a pig squeal with deep Arkansas roots. "I said, I have a brief statement to make." She paused and looked down again at the notecard.

"My beloved husband, Senator Harry Lackland, is recovering from a stroke that he suffered. I fully expect him to be back on his feet soon. Please keep us in your prayers as we continue with his recovery. I hope you will respect my family's privacy through this difficult time. That's all I have to say." She dropped her hands and turned toward the door.

"Are his doctors saying he'll make a full recovery!" a voice shouted, and she turned back to see who was speaking.

Other voices called out. "When did this happen!"

"Which hospital diagnosed the stroke!"

"Is he awake and responding to treatment!"

More questions erupted. Her head snapped back and forth at each query. She took several quick breaths. Her hands started to shake. She stiffened her spine, stomped her foot, and hollered in a voice sure to be heard throughout the neighborhood. "Stop it! You're nothing but a pack of hyenas. I told you already. Harry needs peace and quiet. Now git outta here!"

Beverly Lackland spun around, barreled into her house, and slammed the door.

The majority leader hit the mute button on the TV tuned to CNN's live coverage of the breaking news event and leaned back in his desk chair. "Well, I think that went as well as we could hope." He smiled, glancing at Elise Warnke and then Jon Rostow, who were standing in front of his desk.

Warnke's shoulders slumped. She opened her mouth as Rostow spoke. "I think that's right, Leader. Beverly Lackland sounded like a mama bear guarding her cub. Or maybe a sow with her piglet." He chuckled. "Looks like we dodged a bullet."

Warnke let out a heavy sigh.

"Something bothering you, Elise?" Leader Johnson's face held a new wariness.

"Oh, Charley. I'll be frank. I'm very worried. She's lying. We know she's lying. Yes, we can try to pin the blame on her." She took a step closer to the leader's desk. "But if someone finds out the truth, well, it's most likely going to come back and bite us on our bottoms. And you know the press. She didn't give them any details and she blew up when they tried to ask her legitimate questions. I thought she looked like a woman trying to hide something. And if I think that, you can be sure those—'hyenas,'" she winced, "most of whom are experts in knowing when someone is lying, well, they're going to be thinking the same thing. And you both know when they smell a story, there's no stopping them. They're going to go sniffing around at hospitals."

Rostow unclasped his hands from behind his back and shifted his weight from one foot to the other. The leader's face remained impassive.

"Privacy laws may preclude medical personnel from giving out details, but this is too big a story. And she flat-out lied when she said he's going to make a full recovery. The story's going to leak. And when it does, are we really going to be able to convince the press that we didn't know about this?" She shook her head. "Even if it were the truth, and it isn't, I don't think we've got much chance of that."

"Well, Elise, I've learned not to question your intuition," Johnson replied. "So, we'll just have to keep mum and hope that if this blows up, Beverly's the target. All we have to do is hold this off a week or so, and then it'll be too late for them to influence the election. Early voting has started in most states."

"That's right, Leader," Rostow piped up. "The election results are already baked. People have made up their minds. It's too late for the Republicans to flood the air waves even if they think they've now got a chance. We don't have much to worry about."

Muckrakers Inc., a right-wing organization dedicated to exposing liberal and Democratic scandals, had promised freelance photographer John Lamb a princely sum if he could get a compromising photograph of Senator Lackland. After snapping several shots of Mrs. Lackland and trying to peer inside the house through its first-floor windows, Lamb hadn't come up with the money shot.

The show was over. The gaggle of reporters began to depart. The TV crews were packing up their gear. Lamb leaned against a tall tree in the front yard near the corner of the Lacklands' house. Two dormer windows on the second floor jutted out of the front of the residence. It looked like the curtains were open. He studied the tree limbs and mapped out a route to access the roof.

As soon as the last TV van departed, he slung his camera strap over his shoulder, took a quick look around, and started to climb. It was a little tricky, but he was young and hungry. In no time at all, he swung onto the roof and carefully worked his way along the side of the house over to the window. He looked inside. Just an empty bedroom. He glanced over his shoulder. No one was watching from the street or the nearby houses.

Grabbing the window frame, he swung in front of the window, balancing on the edge of the slippery slate shingles and gutter. No one was there. The roof on the front of the house was quite steep and he plopped to a seat on the opposite side. He inched along until he reached the second dormer. He grabbed the corner of the dormer and gingerly stood up. His right foot slipped a little, but he hung on. He peered around and into the window.

Well, I'll be damned, there's the old guy. Tubes coming out of his arms and mouth. He doesn't look so good. With his right hand, he lifted his camera, positioned it in front of the window, and took several shots.

He sat back down on the roof and reviewed the pictures in the viewfinder. *Alright. What is it the NBA players say? Oh yeah, "I'm gonna get a bag."* He let out a high-pitched giggle and gave a fist pump.

He stood up too quickly and his feet slipped out from under him. Sliding down the roof, he grabbed the gutter with his left hand, which stopped his downward momentum but smashed him against the side of the house. He lost his grip and landed on a large boxwood shrub.

He rolled out of the bush and bolted to his feet as the front door opened. There stood Beverly Lackland.

"I told you to git! I'm calling the cops. Now, git!" she screamed.

Lamb sprinted down the street and around the corner, where his parked car was waiting.

FORTY-THREE

White House

"What do you mean they stopped work on the golf course?" Parker bellowed like an enraged water buffalo, sending a rumble throughout the Oval Office. He had been leaning back in his chair but was now sitting ramrod straight. "They can't do that. Don't they know I'm the president of the United States? Who told them to stop?"

"Mr. President." Steve Simpson stood before the Resolute Desk, where the president was seated. "Judge John Jay issued the stop work order at the request of the Maryland Chapter of the Sierra Club. The group requested an emergency injunction to stop the cutting of the trees and to request the reopening of Catoctin Park. The judge ruled in their favor."

"But it's a matter of national security. He can't do that. I'll issue an executive order insisting they restart work."

"I'm sorry, sir, you can't. With the cancelation of the G-7 meeting, Henry Murphy, the director of the Secret Service, backed off his recommendation to establish a buffer zone between the park and Camp David."

"Get him on the phone. He's fired. Right now. You tell him. I'm not going to allow them to stop me. It's national security, goddamn it. I'm the fucking president. If I say it's national security, that's what it is."

"Sir, I'm sorry. This isn't going the way I planned. Louis Kelleher is the congressman in that part of Maryland and he's on the House Natural Resources Committee. They oversee national parks. Anyway, he's demanding an investigation into the park closing."

"But you said it's, what did you call it? Congress doesn't get involved in these things."

"Yes, sir, continuity of government, sir. In general, the Congress allows the executive branch wide latitude in determining what we need to do to protect the presidency. But Congress reserves the right to review our plans. They just don't usually bother. But in this case, being it's a popular national park and it's in Kelleher's district, and he's on the oversight committee, well, unfortunately, he's not going to let this go quietly. And, sir, since you're doing this to build a golf course, frankly, sir, that won't pass the smell test." Standing stoically with perfect posture and a blank, tight-lipped expression, he stared at the president. "I'm sorry, sir, there's nothing more we can do."

"Oh yeah? I'll show you. I'm going to get my golf course even if I have to send you out there with an axe to chop down the fucking trees."

Steve's posture sagged. He shook his head and sighed. "Mr. President, on another subject." He didn't wait to be told no. "Plans are readied to begin the blockade. Pac fleet has positioned the Carl Vinson Carrier Strike Group near the Philippines. We've deployed a squadron of B-2 bombers at Anderson Air Force Base on Guam. We have special operators with tanker support and two squadrons of F-22 Raptors at Kadena on Okinawa. Our intelligence agencies are positioning overhead assets in the region. In short, we're set to go. But, frankly, sir, the new head of INDOPACOM, Admiral Cooper, is urging you not to enforce a blockade. Even with all this firepower, we'd be quickly outgunned by the Chinese if this turns ugly. And ever since we shot down their spy balloon, the Chinese have had an itchy trigger finger. Sir, despite your beliefs, we still have no evidence, NONE!"—the volume of his voice doubled in an anguished cry, then quickly he regained his composure—"nothing that says the Chinese are involved with the bioweapon. All evidence points to the Russians."

"Putin wouldn't do that."

"I understand you think that. But look at the facts. President Putin has been trying to bolster his borders for a decade. Crimea, Ukraine, threatening the Baltics, et cetera. He's intent on destroying NATO, which he sees as the only thing stopping him from regaining hegemony in the region." He paused, expecting a dismissing comment, but the president remained silent.

"The Russians are justifiably angry and nervous about the expansion of our European alliance. They still remember the Western invasions of Mother Russia, and the particular horror the Nazis unleashed upon Stalingrad. It makes perfect sense for Putin to deploy a bioweapon to force us to back down. Kinetic warfare is messy. Too many Russian soldiers died in the Ukraine. And remember, Afghanistan wasn't just a black eye for the US. Forty years ago, it was also a defeat for the Soviet Union. Modern warfare can be as deadly as the tragedies of World War One and our own Civil War. That's why cyberattacks are on the rise, and why bioweapons, like this coronavirus, are so, um, attractive."

It was clear he wasn't getting through. Time for a new tack. "Besides, we don't really know if Putin is involved. All we know is this group claiming to represent freedom fighters worldwide is behind it. Perhaps, it's the Russian mafia, or Russian oligarchs, but all our intel suggests the virus has been manufactured in Russia. And now we are hearing rumors that it might have escaped the lab."

"So, you're saying that Putin isn't involved? That's what I've been trying to tell you."

Steve felt a glimmer of hope. "Yes, sir, it's possible it's not Putin or his government. But signals are clear it's coming from Russia. Not China. So can we hold off on the blockade?"

"For now."

Steve relaxed. "Yes, sir. That's a very wise decision you're making. I'll pass on the message."

"But you haven't convinced me the Chinese aren't the ones. So keep those forces on alert. And, goddamn it, Simpson, you better figure out how to get me my golf course. Now get your ass out of my office before I fire it."

"Thank you, Mr. President." Steve bowed quickly, turned, and left. *Well, I'll be damned. I'm not sure how that worked. But thank God it did. I'd say I earned my salary today. But that effing golf course is going to be the death of me.*

FORTY-FOUR

Dirksen Senate Office Building

Paula sat at the small desk surrounded by safes in the closet-sized secure office. She reached for the receiver on her secure phone, took a deep breath, and punched in the number Al Gianini had given her. "Good morning, I guess it is for you, sir. Um, sir, you don't know me, but my name is Paula Means. I'm the, um, staff director, of the Senate's Appropriations Defense Subcommittee. Al Gianini gave me your number. He's an old friend." Paula cringed that she was cold-calling the commander of the Indo-Pacific Command as well as neglecting to use her married name. She'd also called herself staff director, which is how Pentagon officials referred to the individual in her job role even though the proper title is clerk. That was a misnomer frequently corrected by the committee's actual staff director, Pat Sistrunk.

"Actually, Ms. Means, I'm well aware of who you are. You probably don't remember, but we met a decade ago in Brussels when you were traveling with your boss, Senator Mitsunaga. I was SACEUR's aide-de-camp. Besides, you're famous here in Hawaii. What can I do for you?"

Paula racked her brain for a remembrance of Admiral Cooper from that trip and vaguely recalled an image of a tall, trim, sandy-haired navy captain with a winning smile. She chuckled, "Well, you've come a long way since then, sir. Congratulations on your fourth star and assuming your current post. And, please, call me Paula. But why did you say I was famous? Because of my work on behalf of Senator Mitsunaga?"

"Well, sure, I guess that's part of it, but mostly for the Second Battle of Pearl Harbor, as we call it. There's actually a case study at the Navy War College in Rhode Island that examines that event. It discusses how we used sensor fusing to defeat the North Korean attack. And it gives you great credit for coming up with the idea and, without exaggerating, saving Hawaii. So, that's the main reason you're famous in this office."

"Gee, sir, I think they might be overstating my role."

"Not according to one of my predecessors, Admiral Lockwood. He credits you and Al Gianini, too, for tamping down the war rhetoric with the Chinese. So, what I can do for you, Paula?"

"Sir, let me first apologize for calling out of the blue, but it's extremely important and classified. Could we go secure?"

"Of course. Hold one."

Paula looked down at the small digital screen on her bulky desktop phone. After a few seconds it noted the unit was now secure. "Admiral, Al Gianini suggested I call you directly. I'm not trying to overstate this, but it's a matter of extreme urgency. At the request of my former boss, Senator Mitsunaga, I have been in contact with an Israeli man, who I believe is Mossad. He spoke with me a few weeks ago to tell me that Israel believed the Russians were readying the use of a new bioweapon against the West. He said it's fashioned to look like a very lethal form of coronavirus. Since then, we've all seen the deadly evidence of this weapon and been subjected to blackmail from a group claiming to be terrorists." She took a quick breath and plunged on.

"Sir, this is obviously extremely sensitive. I was told that the Israelis have an agent inside the weapons lab where the virus and its antidote were manufactured. They had planned to expose the Russian operation once they were sure they could stop it but have had to change their strategy. Apparently, the North Koreans were able to acquire some amount of the virus—"

"Ms. Means, Paula, stop right there. As you probably know, the White House insists the Russians aren't involved. I suspect you may know that we've mustered our forces in the western Pacific to conduct an operation targeting the Chinese. I can't go into any more details, I'm sure you understand, but my orders are to prepare to prosecute that action. My hands are tied." He took a deep breath. "But we also have intel that correlates closely with what you're saying. We have no idea what the North Koreans are up to, but from the chatter we've picked up, it's reasonable to assume they have the weapon."

Paula smiled. "It might be odd to say, but I'm relieved that you think the North Koreans have this deadly virus only because it adds to the veracity of the Israeli claims. The Israelis now are planning to steal the vaccine from the Russian lab and transport it across the border into Kazakhstan. Which is where you might come in."

"How's that, Paula?"

"Sir, if the Israelis are able to secure the vaccine and get it safely out of Russia, they'll need someone to transport it from Kazakhstan to the US, to Fort Detrick, Maryland. Our army experts there can figure out its chemical components and start the manufacturing process. If the Koreans have the virus, it's critical that we begin this as quickly as possible." Paula scrunched up her nose and after a moment's hesitation continued. "Perhaps, sir, and I don't mean to overstate my, um, sir, what I'm trying to ask is could you send a C-17 to retrieve the vaccine and carry it to DC?" She picked up her pace, as if that might somehow minimize the audacity of her request. "Congress gave you funding to conduct a global reach exercise. Could you use some of those funds to carry out an operation with tanker support and secure the vaccine? I mean, I'm not trying to tell you how to do your job. I mean, with all due respect, sir, but this is vital and Al Gianini said you offered to help. Sir?"

"I'm not sure how that's possible. Kazakhstan isn't in my area of responsibility. It's under CENTCOM."

"Yes, sir, I know, but . . ."

"And we don't have any bases in the area. Nothing even close. We shut down everything as Iraq and Afghanistan wound down. And the Kazakhs aren't really allies."

"Well, yes, sir, all that's true. But we do have a relationship with their military under the international military education and training program and under our overseas disaster and humanitarian assistance program. With that terrible tragedy with the virus in eastern Kazakhstan, they might be open to a disaster mitigation training operation."

She couldn't keep more words from tumbling out of her mouth. "We've also trained some of their senior officers. And we worked closely with them after the collapse of the Soviet Union in dismantling their nuclear weapons programs. I remember Al Gianini talking about getting to know their army's chief of staff when he was still on active duty." She gulped a breath.

"Sir, I know I'm rambling, and I apologize, but all it would take is to get clearance to land at one of their civilian airports and pick up the vaccine. You could describe it as a planning exercise to be ready to provide humanitarian assistance if there were a disaster in the region. They are prone to severe flooding and frankly are probably due for a large earthquake. You know, I'd never have considered raising this if we weren't facing such an incredible threat. Sir?"

"Well, assuming you're right that we have funding for a global reach exercise, and assuming CENTCOM would be okay with us conducting an exercise in their region, and assuming the Kazakhs would let us land, I guess it's conceivable. But I'm not sure how we could put that together in time to conduct what amounts to a rescue operation." She could hear the keys clicking on his computer and he continued.

"I've got C-17s in the western Pacific and tankers, but I'd still need additional tanking from CENTCOM and . . ."

"Yes, sir. CENTCOM's got tankers at Incirlik, in Turkey."

"That's right. I tell you what. I'll call CENTCOM commander Frank Munson in Tampa and see if he could lay on tanker support for a snap exercise. But I don't know how we'll get clearance to land in Kazakhstan."

"Let me work on that. And, sir, I hate to say it, but we really need to do this no later than tomorrow."

"But what if your information is incorrect and there's no vaccine in Kazakhstan?"

"Well, Admiral, look at it like this. It's a great way to practice global reach."

FORTY-FIVE

Sverdlovsk Oblast, Russia

"Quickly! Hide the motorcycle and get in the back of the car." A bald middle-aged man whispered instructions out the car window even though it was nighttime and they were in the middle of nowhere on the highway shoulder at the edge of a dense forest. "Lie down and pull the seat down over top of you."

Aaron did as he was told. "Where are you taking me?" he asked, propping himself up on one elbow and leaving the seat cracked open so he could hear and see the back of the man's head.

"Quiet! Do you have the vaccine?"

"Yes."

The man smashed the accelerator, lifted his satellite phone, and spoke. "I have the package. It will take us a few hours to reach the border and another two to get to the Kostanay Airport. Have you arranged transport?"

Aaron struggled to make out what the person on the other end of the phone was saying. Then he heard the call end abruptly.

"Ayye. The old man's a fool." The driver spat the words. "Still no way out of Kazakhstan. He says to trust him. Trust? How can we trust when we are hundreds of kilometers from the border with a pack of dogs on our trail?"

Jesus Christ. What a mess. At least get me out of Russia.

"Try to get some sleep, Aaron. You will need to be rested for whatever fate has in store."

Aaron lay flat on the floorboards and let the seat fall on top of him. He spied a latch that would secure the seat, but left it open. In the darkness, with the rumble of the car's engine beneath him, he found himself drifting off to sleep.

The car's brakes screeched, forcing Aaron against the front of the seat as the car rapidly decelerated. Then his head bashed against the side as the car jerked hard to the right.

"They found us! Aaron, take this."

Something went thud on the floor in front of him. Aaron peeked out. It was quite dark, but he spotted the satellite phone. He grabbed it, slipped it inside his jacket, and pulled the seat down and locked it.

"Don't say a word. Dare to breathe, Aaron, and good luck. The fate of the world depends upon you. Shalom."

Aaron was tossed around, bashing against all sides of his coffin-like hiding place. He crashed against the seat above him as the car went airborne. "Fucking great way to die," he muttered. He heard what sounded like the scrape of tree branches against the car, and then *boom!*, the car slammed into something; the horn blared for a few seconds and then trailed off to silence.

He lay on his back, his heart pounding. He slowly pulled his pistol from his jacket pocket and unzipped the other to check the vaccine. The pocket was dry. All good. Except for whoever was out there waiting for him. Well, if they tried to pull him out, they'd have a rude awakening.

Voices shouted in Russian. Aaron picked up a few words and heard footfalls outside. The voices got louder. He understood "Get out of the car!" The man in the driver's seat didn't answer or move. Again, voices demanded the driver exit the vehicle. No response.

The voices got louder and angrier. Still nothing. Shots blasted into the body of the vehicle. Aaron could hear glass breaking. Then, "He's dead," and something about an old man.

The car swayed as they tried to pry open the door. He thought he caught the word "broken." Footsteps trampled all around the car amid a cacophony of voices, all shouting. He cringed as he recognized the sound of the trunk opening.

"Suitcase. . . . No Arab."

Aaron took in a quiet breath and, using both hands, pointed his pistol at the seat above him. *I'm next.*

Distant sirens were growing louder. He heard them click off and more car doors being opened and slammed. "Where is he?" a woman shrieked in Russian.

Could it be? More footsteps approached.

"Who is that old man? Where's the Arab?" the female voice questioned.

"No Arab. We shot this one. Escaping," a voice answered.

"You fools. Poison!" she screamed.

A man asked something about the virus, his voice trembling.

"No. Cyanide," the woman replied. "Where is the vaccine?"

"No vaccine in the trunk."

"Search him."

He felt them pulling on the car door again.

"Fools!" again the woman shouted. The sound of more broken glass. Then the car tilted to the left as if someone was climbing in through the window.

A familiar lilac scent crept into the cramped compartment where he hid. It was her. It had to be.

Muffled sounds. Was someone searching the man's pockets?

"Nothing," she called out and then let loose a blood-curdling scream of frustration that made him flinch. His boot softly thumped against the seat.

Did she hear that? He gripped the pistol tighter. Silence. He could hear her breathing as if she was leaning over the front seat. He waited. The lilac scent grew stronger. *Looks like she'll have to die after all.* Someone was running their hand over the seat. They tried to lift it up. Then silence.

The fragrance faded. "He's not here. Let's go."

"What do we do with this one?" a man's voice asked.

"Leave him!" Aaron heard her voice shouting instructions away from the car as footfalls grew quieter. "Come back in the morning and get him and the car. The Arab is still out here somewhere. We must hurry."

FORTY-SIX

Dirksen Senate Office Building

"I don't know how you got us clearance to land in Kazakhstan, Paula, but we're good to go. I've got a C-17 gassed up on the runway at Kadena on Okinawa. Tanker support is arranged for refueling before he gets to the, um, Kostanay Airport, I guess it is."

Paula smiled and leaned back in her chair behind her desk. "Well, sir, that's great. The Israelis say they have the vaccine and it's on its way to the Kostanay Airport."

"CENTCOM has laid on more tankers as he's coming out of Central Asia. We've even got EUCOM sending tanker support from the UK to Central Europe and down the Atlantic coast for a last refueling coming out of the Med. What's the word on your end?"

"Perfect. The tankers are essential, sir. The Kazakhs agreed to let us land, but they offered no fuel or other support. And they only want us to land and take off again. As far as getting the package on board, well, we'll just have to wing it. I imagine there'll be some confusion or excitement when the C-17 comes rumbling in. We'll have to count on the Israelis to do their part. But, frankly, sir, if the Israelis can steal the vaccine and get out of Russia, I'm pretty sure they'll be able to figure a way to get it aboard the plane."

"Well, I've got to hand it to you, it's all pretty remarkable that we're this far along. I'll greenlight the bird for takeoff and keep my fingers crossed."

Paula leaned forward. "To answer your first question, Admiral Cooper, it was a team effort led primarily by Al Gianini, who reached out to his contacts in the Kazakh military. That and an old friend, Johnny Taylor, who is big in the disaster management business, contacted the emergency preparedness people in Kazakhstan. He told them our plan to practice a snap humanitarian relief mission in case there's a natural disaster or another coronavirus attack."

"Makes sense. Let me know if you hear anything else and I'll tell you when we've got the package and have cleared Kazakh airspace."

Paula started to hang up.

"Oh yeah, Paula, one last question?" she heard him say. "The folks in DC ready to do their magic on the vaccine?"

"Yes, sir. Fort Detrick has been advised that it's coming. I think they're a bit skeptical that this will happen. But they promise they're prepared to work 24/7 to figure it out and get word to the drug companies on the recipe."

"I'm sure we all share the skepticism, Paula. But if this is what it takes, then we got to give it a shot."

"Roger that, sir. I'll let you know if I hear anything."

FORTY-SEVEN

Sverdlovsk Oblast, Russia

Aaron lay waiting, listening. It had been about two hours since the last vehicles had departed, but that didn't mean it was safe. By his calculation, it must be nearing dawn. They'd be coming soon to tow the damaged car. He had to get away now.

He grabbed the sliding latch and eased it open. *Careful now.* Using both hands while still clutching his pistol, he raised the seat above him a crack. He was right. The first rays of a pale winter sunrise reflected off the broken glass on the car floor. *It's now or never.*

He lifted the seat just enough for him to slide out onto the floor. A whiff of stinking Russian cigarette smoke. *Bad luck.* On the other hand, it could mean a vehicle nearby. Only way to get to the border in time because this car wasn't going anywhere. *The vaccine's been warming up for four hours. What did she say? It's only good for twelve to twenty-four hours. Let's hope it's the latter.*

Aaron got to his knees and peeked out the window on the passenger's side in the direction of the cigarette odor. A glowing ember lit up the silhouette of a helmeted figure in an olive drab uniform relaxing on a motorcycle. Aaron looked to his left, right, and behind him. *That's it. Just the one guard.*

He raised his pistol and aimed for the guard's torso. The helmet made a head shot too risky. Aaron fired three shots in rapid succession. The first was a little high and caught the man in the neck. As his body twisted, the second found the man's chest. The third ripped through his crotch as he and motorcycle went sprawling.

With pistol in one hand, Aaron dove out the car window, rolled over and up into a crouch position. All quiet. He ran over to the Russian lying on the ground. Dead. He stuck his pistol in his waistband, then removed the man's helmet and dragged the body over to the car by the jacket collar. The trunk was still open. Aaron lifted the dead guard and rolled him into the trunk and slammed it.

He stood the motorcycle up, pulled out the satellite phone, and turned it on.

"This is Aaron, who's this?"

"Aaron, my son, it's good to hear your voice. Where are you?"

His mentor's familiar voice rekindled the disgust he felt toward the old man with the cavalier disregard for human life. "Your agent is dead. He killed himself. I evaded capture. I'm guessing I'm near the border. I've got wheels, but there's a problem."

"Is the vaccine safe?"

Aaron reached in his pocket. No sign of moisture. "Yes, but that's the problem."

"What? Why?"

"Because we're running short on time. The vaccine must be kept frozen. It doesn't last long once it's reached room temperature. Maybe another eight or ten hours. Plus your agent here said something about an airport."

"Yes, Kostanay Airport. I've arranged an American military transport for you."

"But then what? By the time we get the vaccine to a lab it could be too late. Your bomb didn't just take out the virus, it eliminated the supply of vaccine. I might have all that's left. I think we need to focus on stopping Kim, the North Korean who has a vial of the virus. That's the only solution."

"I see. That's unfortunate. You need to focus on your part. Get out of Russia and to that airport. It's a couple-hour drive from the border. We'll just have to hope the vaccine lasts longer than you think."

Aaron hung up, stuffed the phone inside his jacket, and climbed on the motorcycle. "This is ridiculous. Kim's out there somewhere," he grumbled. "He can destroy the world."

FORTY-EIGHT

South Pacific

The swaying motion stopped as the submersible was lowered from the Liberia-registered freighter. The impact of it hitting the water jostled his body roughly. He lay flat on his back, ready for the three-hour journey. A single bulb lit his surroundings in a dim glow.

He was already feeling the effect of the virus: throbbing head, hellacious cough, and difficulty getting sufficient air into his lungs. His ears popped as the sub sank to a hundred-foot depth. The surge of the diesel-powered engine pushed him forward.

It was cold. The craft provided little insulation from the South Pacific Ocean waters, which might be balmy at the surface, but not at this depth. His gaudy flowered bathing suit, similar to suits worn by tourists to the Hawaiian Islands, did little to keep him warm.

The sub's course had been programmed with the aid of GPS. He'd hit the coast of Kauai at Barking Sands, the home of the navy's Pacific Missile Range Facility. He tried to relax and accept the effects of the virus. He reached in his pocket and fingered the capped syringe that held the lifesaving antidote. He'd stolen it, too, from the Russian facility and had kept it in his pocket for two days . He'd inject it into his bloodstream as soon as he'd infected the American military.

His was a simple mission. Simply get out of the sub in the surf, walk onto the beach, seek assistance as the deadly virus ran its course, and breathe on as many sailors as he could find before stabbing himself with the vaccine. Then all he had to do was wait for them to spread the deadly virus and die. He knew once the infected left the beach, they'd transmit the disease first to the people on Kauai, then to the neighboring islands and then to the American mainland via airplanes departing Lihue Airport.

His nation would remain secure within its borders and wait out the plague as it spread around the world. Surely, the Russians would supply the lifesaving vaccine to his people as Americans, Japanese, and Europeans perished in mass numbers. Perhaps even the bourgeois Chinese leadership would be wiped out. North Korea might then rule all of Asia. *All glory to our founder the Great Leader, his son the Dear Leader, and now our Supreme Leader, Kim Jong Un.*

He chuckled thinking of the poor bastards, his unfortunate countrymen, on the freighter that he'd infected before setting sail on this mini sub. One day their floundering vessel would be found with no one alive to tell the story. By then, it would be far too late to stop him. And when fingers were pointed at North Korea, his nation would claim they were hoodwinked by the Anti-Imperialist terrorists. After all, they'd say, North Korea would never sacrifice its own sailors.

With minimal room to move, Kim passed the time by wiggling his feet in time to patriotic Korean folk songs he'd learned as a child. It hadn't seemed like three hours when he felt the submarine rise in the water. Finally, he felt the bumping of the sub as it found the Hawaiian shoreline and bobbed to the surface.

His head throbbing, Kim took a deep breath and opened the hatch. Warm tropical water flowed into the boat and he floated out. The sub filled with water and sank in the surf, about ten yards from the shore.

A man fishing on the shoreline saw him emerge from the water coughing and wearing only swimming trunks. This man sloshed over to Kim waving his hands and shaking his head. "No come ashore. *Kapu.* Forbidden. This Niihau. No one come. Go." He pointed toward the ocean.

Kim staggered to the beach and fell into the arms of the Native Hawaiian fisherman. He blurted out the only English words he knew, "Help me." Delirium was overtaking him, but he managed to pull out the syringe from his swimsuit pocket and jab his leg.

He laughed and coughed simultaneously and dropped the syringe into the surf. He looked over the fisherman's shoulder. *Where are the others? This old man doesn't look military. No wonder the Americans are so weak. They have no discipline. Long live the Democratic People's Republic.*

Kim had been told the vaccine would reverse the effects of the virus as soon as it hit his bloodstream, but he only felt worse. The old man dragged him away from the water and laid him on the beach.

Then the old man got on a bicycle and rode away.

Keoni Kanehale stashed his fishing pole up the beach a ways away from the stranger and pulled his bicycle from the beach grass. Today, only he and his wife had stayed behind on Niihau to keep watch over the island. The hundred or so other residents of their village of Puuwai were on Kauai getting COVID booster shots and supplies.

"Ella!" he shouted, calling his wife by her nickname as he peddled the sandy track to the village. "An outsider swam ashore and seems very sick. We must radio Kauai for a helicopter to rescue him."

FORTY-NINE

Dirksen Senate Office Building

"Admiral Cooper? It's Paula. Sir, we have a problem. The Israelis just informed me that their agent who has the vaccine has had trouble getting to the airport and is delayed."

"Roger, that. I'll have the C-17 remain on station and orbit the region a little longer. Do we have a specific window to get in and out of the airport?"

"Well, no, sir, not exactly."

"Then that's what we'll do. I laid on extra tanker support from Incirlik. So I got plenty of fuel. Just let me know when we're good to go."

"Yes, sir, but the problem is the Israelis believe the vaccine can't survive at room temperature for more than something like twenty-four hours. Maybe even less."

"What you're telling me is that by the time I pick it up and fly it to DC, it'll be useless? I'd need a rocket ship to meet that schedule."

"Unfortunately, that's right, sir." But an idea lit up her mind.

"I'll recall the birds. No reason to waste gas on a wild goose chase, then."

The phone went silent for a moment and Paula thought frantically how to broach the subject. "Sir, um, if possible, could you wait to call off the exercise? I got an idea. I'll be back in touch soon. Goodbye."

Paula hung up and scrolled through her cell phone contacts. "Kelly, Kelly, Kelly," she muttered. She found the contact under "Skunk" for Lockheed's Advanced Development Programs, its famous Skunk Works laboratory in the high desert of Southern California. She pushed back from her desk, ran out of her office and through the interior corridor to the SCIF. She punched in a bunch of numbers, heard the door unlock, ran in, and picked up the phone. "C'mon, Rich, be there . . ."

"Kelly."

"Mr. Kelly, this is Paula, um, Means, sir. I work for the Senate Ap—"

"Paula! What a surprise! I heard you'd moved to Hawaii. How's paradise?"

"Sir, I'm back in DC now, in my old job. I got a crazy question to ask you. It might get into some classified things. Can you go secure?"

"Yeah, sure. Wait one."

Paula listened as the phone clicked and static crackled. The all-clear sign popped up on the display. "You there, sir?"

"Yep, what can I do for you?"

"Like I said, crazy question. Your guys at the Skunk Works got any hot, new prototype aircraft that can get around the world really fast? I've read the stories in *Aviation Week* speculating that Lockheed's building an SR-72 or Aurora or some other hypersonic plane right out of *Star Wars*. Is any of that true?"

"So, before I begin, did you say you're back on the committee?"

"Yes, sir. Back as the clerk on the Defense Subcommittee. I've got all the tickets, sir. Have you got something like that?"

"Short answer, no."

Paula's shoulders slumped. *Well, that's that. I guess we have no way to get the vaccine in time.* She perked up. "Wait. Is there a long answer? Something that might do the trick?"

"Paula, the only thing with that kind of speed is the old SR-71 itself. What are you trying to do?"

"Oh, sir. It's kinda crazy, but the Israelis got ahold of the antidote to this new virus. The one the Anti-Imperialist terrorist group's threatening to unleash on the world. The problem is, it's on its way to Kazakhstan, but it loses its potency, or whatever the right word is, in a day or so out of deep freeze. And by the time we get a transport plane there to pick it up, well, we'd have no way to get it to our scientists in time. So I called you in case there is something that could complete that mission. But I guess we're out of luck."

"That's quite a story. Heh, heh. But, you know, I do have an SR-71 in the barn."

"What? I thought they were all in museums or chopped up or something. Can she still fly?"

"Oh yeah. My maintenance guru Big Willie Lanier and I take her out of bubble wrap every few months and fire up the engines. In fact we did that earlier today. She's still got it."

"Really? Could you fly it to Kazakhstan and then to DC? How long would it take to get ready? Could you pull the whole thing off in less than twelve hours, or thereabouts?"

"It's not that simple, Paula," he said slowly, drawing out the considerations. "For a mission like that, flying almost all the way around the world, she'd need to refuel a few times. No one's done anything like that in more than twenty years. And I'd have to preposition fuel. I don't think that's feasible. The infrastructure isn't there to pull it off. Yeah, I could get the bird off the ground, and gas it up once using my limited resources here at Palmdale. But she'd need fuel somewhere like Hawaii or Alaska, depending on your route, and certainly by the time she got near Japan, and somewhere around Central Asia, and maybe over the Atlantic. Where would we get those assets? Besides, she doesn't take normal jet fuel. She was built to fly on JP-7. I still got some, and there might be some in old tanks at US Air Force bases around the world, but it's unlikely. And you need the old KC-135Q or KC-10 tankers. They're the only birds set up to refuel the Blackbird."

Paula's mind whirred as she listened to the litany of obstacles. "Well, I might be able to get tankers," she offered. "I think the 135s were remanned into the 'RT' variant, if someone knows where there might be stores of JP-7 . . ."

"Well, there's one other minor problem." Kelly took in a large gulp of air and exhaled. "I don't have a pilot qualified to do such a mission. The pilot I use can take off, fly around a little, and land, but no way could he do aerial refueling and that highly strenuous mission."

"You don't think there's any old air force guys around who used to fly her?"

"Well, yeah, sure, but other than a retiree or two, I wouldn't know how to get in touch with them. Besides, flying the SR-71 takes incredible training and practice and stamina. Only guy I know who could pull off something like that is Balls to the Wall."

"Who did you say?"

"Heh, heh. Yeah, I said balls to the wall, Paula. Pardon my French. His real name is Butch Boswald. Former air force major. Crazy surfer dude who loved to fly fast. His nickname was Balls to the Wall."

"Could you find him? I mean, we're talking about the survival of humanity here."

"Holy cow, Paula. I can't believe we're even talking about this. It's crazy."

"If there's any shot at all, we got to grab it, sir."

"I got a number that might work. But, trust me, the logistics are way harder than me getting Boswald."

"Sir, I'll work on the logistics if you can find me the pilot."

FIFTY

White House

Steve Simpson walked softly into the president's dining room. "Mr. President, we have a situation developing." The chief executive was seated in an upholstered gold brocade chair at a large square walnut table enjoying a late dinner of ketchup-drenched steak and french fries.

The president looked up with a frown, a dab of ketchup on his chin. "Goddamn it, Simpson, can't I even eat in peace?"

"Sorry, sir. It's just that it looks like we might have a breakout of the terrorist virus on a small private island in Hawaii," Steve continued without giving the boss a chance to object. "The navy is reporting that a man came ashore on the island of Niihau suffering from serious respiratory problems. He died shortly after arriving while the folks who found him had gone for help."

"So, a guy dies on the beach. Why do you think it's the virus?"

"Yes, sir, well, they're reporting that the gentleman who discovered him is now showing similar symptoms. Our experts at the Centers for Disease Control fear it's the virus. We've quarantined the island. Luckily, there are only two people, besides the dead Asian man, on the island."

"Ah-ha, Mr. Smarty-Pants, he's Chinese, just like I told you. Now, get that goddamn blockade set up and tell the Chinese they stop this now or we'll get serious."

"Yes, sir. You can do that, sir, but you should know Israeli intelligence suspects the infected man is a terrorist out of North Korea, not China. They believe the North Koreans stole the virus from the Russians."

"Jesus Christ, Simpson, how stupid are you? You can't trust the Israelis and, besides, Putin wouldn't let them do that to me. Carry out my orders. NOW!" Parker glared at him.

Steve paused before answering, "Yes, sir, I'll tell the Pentagon. But—"

"No buts, Simpson, do it."

"Yes, sir."

FIFTY-ONE

Southern California

"Is that you, Balls to the Wall? Sounds like you're in a wind tunnel."

"Who the hell is this?" Butch Boswald barked into his cell phone. "No one calls me that anymore!" He kept his gaze on the horizon while flying the single-engine Cessna aircraft.

"It's Rich Kelly, Boz. Where are you?"

"Just took off from Malibu, heading for Half Moon Bay. There's a storm off the coast that's stirring up epic forty-foot waves at Maverick's tomorrow. I'm heading up for a weekend of surfing my ass off. What the hell are you calling me for, Kelly?"

"I guess this means you're still flight qualified. It's a good thing. I got a mission for you."

"A mission? What are you talking about? I'm retired."

"I need a Blackbird pilot who's effing crazy and you're the first guy I thought of." Boz could hear the smile on Kelly's face.

"Blackbird? What the hell? What Blackbird? They're all junked," Boz shouted over the engine noise. "You takin' to day drinking? 'Cause you sure ain't making sense."

Kelly took a more sober tone. "I'm deadly serious, Boz. I kept a Blackbird and it's ready to go. Washington needs us to pick up a package in Kazakhstan and get it to some DC scientists pronto. You're about the only guy around who might be able to pull this off."

"Fly around the world? And land in Kazakhstan? You really are certifiable."

"Boz, I'm serious. You know that virus those terrorists are threatening to use on us? Well, our friends in DC have access to the antidote, but it's in Kazakhstan, and probably already degrading, and they need to get it to the lab ASAP. Frankly, you're our only hope of pulling this off. It's for the good of the world, really. And I know you got to be a little crazy to try it, but, seriously, Boz, you were always more than a little crazy. So, change your heading and fly that plane here to Palmdale. I got the Blackbird gassed up and ready."

"This is nuts."

"Yeah, but it'll be a lot more fun than riding waves."

FIFTY-TWO

Dirksen Senate Office Building

"So, bottom line, Paula, we still got enough supply of JP-7 to support an SR-71 mission. The bean counters decided it was cheaper to store it on our bases overseas than get past all the environmental restrictions to get rid of it. Problem is the location of the fuel."

Paula was at the small desk in the Defense Subcommittee's SCIF. She hunched over the secure phone, nervously glancing at her watch every few seconds. Her blonde hair hung down past her shoulders and she was constantly tucking the loose strands behind her ears. "Can you explain that, Admiral?"

"Yes. We've got a small dump here in Hawaii in a secure tank at Hickam. My guys say it might be enough to refuel a Blackbird, but that's about it. We've got a larger supply in Okinawa at Kadena, but other than that, you got to go all the way to Turkey to get refueled and then England. So, I could probably get an SR-71 all the way to Kazakhstan, but I can't get him out. I'm afraid we're out of luck. Besides we're about to get real busy here in the Pacific. I'm sorry, but I need to recall the aircraft."

"Are you sure, sir? I mean, with all due respect, this is the last chance we have to stop this madness." She paused and heard a heavy sigh on the other end.

Feeling like she was pushing her luck, she continued. "Sir, I just thought of something. By any chance you got one of the special 135s out of McConnell in Japan? You know, the ones that do special ops and that can be refueled midair? They can carry JP-7, and with tanker support, they can fly a long time and fly through restricted airspace if need be."

"I can't go into details, Paula, but yes, I have a couple RTs on the ground in theater. But what good does that do?"

"Sir, couldn't you load one up with JP-7, fly it at top speed toward Kazakhstan, and meet up with the SR-71 before it goes into Kazakh airspace, and then top it off coming out on its way to DC?"

"Yeah, that's possible. But I can't refuel a privately owned aircraft unless somebody reimburses me. That SR-71 isn't Air Force. It's Lockheed's."

"Gee, sir. I can't ask Lockheed to pay for it. But couldn't you use your Emergency and Extraordinary Expenses line? All that's required is for the secretary of the air force to certify the expense is necessary, and you can spend that money on anything!"

"Paula, no way we could get SECAF to sign off on this in time. I'm sorry."

"Maybe you could do it under the rubric of humanitarian assistance? Heck, you bring tons of supplies to people after hurricanes and earthquakes. How's that any different from refueling an SR-71 that's trying to save the world from plague?"

"Hah. You're amazing." The admiral's voice held an unexpected note of admiration and relief. He didn't seem to mind that she had an answer for his every objection. "Anybody ever win an argument with you?"

Paula could sense her cheeks blushing. "Not according to my husband," she timidly mumbled. "So, what do you think?"

"Okay, Paula. Here's what I'll do. I'll authorize one of the special tankers to fly out of Japan toward Kazakh. He can refuel the Blackbird. I've got to recall the other birds out there, but I'll arrange the CENTCOM tanker to top off the RT wherever their paths cross. And I'll instruct the RT to wait inside Kazakhstan for the SR to take off. But if the Blackbird doesn't make it before the tanker needs to return to Japan, we won't wait. That's the best I can do."

"That's great, sir! I'll let Rich Kelly at Lockheed know. Thank you— so much—Admiral. And, sir, um, one last thing: Could you call EUCOM and switch out the fuel they're carrying to JP-7?"

"Okay, I'll do that, but now I need one favor."

"Yes, sir. Name it."

"When your Government Accountability Office comes to audit my books, you tell them this was your idea and you said that we were using the appropriations that you provided legally and with the direct approval of your committee."

Paula smiled. "Of course! I'll do my best, sir. But if you pull this off, you're going to be a hero and GAO won't be a problem. That I can assure you."

FIFTY-THREE

Palmdale, California

The Blackbird was sitting on the tarmac at Palmdale's Plant 41 facility in the California high desert north of LA. The black 107-foot-long aircraft looked just as Boz remembered except that the name LOCKHEED was painted on the tail in bright white letters. The SR-71s were built in the mid-1960s, making this bird more than fifty years old. But she looked brand new.

Somehow Boz had squeezed into the flight suit that Lockheed's pilot used. He'd tucked his long gray locks into a red, white, and blue skullcap, and he was freshly shaven, the skin where his beard had been ghostly pale in contrast to the tan on his cheeks and forehead. Boz turned to look at the Skunk Works director as they walked toward the SR-71. "So, tell me again how this works without the old space suits and helmets? This is just an ordinary flight suit," he said, plucking at the thin Nomex material at his chest. "How am I gonna survive at altitude?"

"The SR-71 cockpit is pressurized to twenty-six thousand feet just like in the old days. You'll still need oxygen, but the old gear was in case something went wrong and you lost cabin pressure."

"Exactly."

"Well, we just have to assume nothing is going to go wrong. I mean, this isn't a recon mission. You won't be snapping pictures of some Russian or Chinese sensitive site."

Boz climbed up the ladder to get in the aircraft and turned to see Kelly following right behind. "You know, this is crazy, Rich."

"I guess so, Boz. But what choice do we have?"

Boz sank into the pilot's seat and looked around. "What the hell is all this?"

"She looks good, don't she?" Kelly beamed. "All-new glass cockpit. I've been using her to test out some new gear, state-of-the-art stuff that's not really ready for prime time. Anyway, Corporate agreed to upgrade the cockpit so I have a better interface for plugging in new components. The latest is a whiz-bang automatic countermeasures dispenser system," he said, pointing to a small digital control display unit. "It picks up any threat and optimizes its response to pop off flares, chaff, or other new-fangled gizmos at the precise moment when it can best spoof an incoming missile. Haven't really tested it out, but our smart guys say it's kickass."

"Well, I'll be damned." Boz's eyes scanned the rest of the controls. "Not sure what good any of that does, but as long as you haven't slowed her down, it should all work out."

"So, you'll take off and tank after liftoff, and fly straight to Hawaii. At Hickam, they'll refuel you and top you off after takeoff. One problem, though." Rich looked Boz in the eye. "It's virtually impossible that the flight crew in the air force tankers will have ever tanked anything like a Blackbird. So, it's gonna be real tricky. From what I've been told, it was never easy, but you're gonna have to do it with green crews."

Boz waved him off. "Yeah, it's not all that different from refueling any other aircraft. As long as they can dangle a hose, I can get the gas."

Rich shrugged. "Okay. If you say so. After that, it's a stretch, but the next stop is Kadena on Okinawa."

"Been there hundreds of times. Know it well."

"Right, same drill. Refuel, take off, and top off the tanks." Kelly took a deep breath and grabbed Boz's shoulder. "Okay, here's where it gets real tricky." He stopped talking until Boz locked eyes with him. "You're going to head straight to Kazakhstan. You probably could make it on one tank of gas, but then you'd be stuck there. We have nowhere to land in the area, except at the . . ." he paused to look at his notes, "the Kostanay Airport, near the Russian border. We're gonna have to refuel you again in-flight."

"Where are we supposed to refuel?"

"Hah, well that's the wrinkle. We don't know. A tanker left Kadena, heading west. I was told it's a special bird that can fly pretty much undetected, tank you, and actually be refueled midair as well."

"Well, I'll be damned!" Boz slapped his thigh. "I heard rumors about those tankers. They're special ops. Got some fancy-ass electronic gear on them. But how the hell am I supposed to find this bird?"

"They'll find you. They know your flight plan. We figure they'll try to hook up in the eastern part of Kazakhstan or, more likely, Mongolia. They'll gas you up and follow you. They'll give you another load when you come out of the airport. We have a bird flying out of England prepared to refuel you over Germany, just in case, and another one in the Atlantic to give you enough gas to make it to DC."

"Jesus, if this works, it'll be a miracle."

"Yeah, well, that's what we need at this point."

FIFTY-FOUR

South Pacific

Boz found his comfort zone at eighty thousand feet flying at nearly twenty-two hundred miles per hour. He couldn't believe the old bird could cruise at this speed without shaking apart on him. It was a real tribute to the Skunk Works team. And proof that the SR-71 program never should have been scrapped, he figured.

He spotted Hawaii and radioed Inouye International Airport. The airport shared runways with Joint Base Pearl Harbor–Hickam, a bastardized facility that combined air force and navy bases in a head-scratching attempt to reduce costs. He was cleared to land and directed to a secluded spot on the air force base once he touched down. He didn't even get out of the plane while she was gassed up. In less than twenty minutes, he was refueled and given clearance for takeoff.

One thousand miles off the coast of Hawaii, a KC-10 tanker radioed to say it was circling waiting to top him off. The operator sounded like he was twelve years old. *Here we go, first test of a green crew.*

Boz remembered the drill: approach the boom and dip your wings to make the mating go smoothly.

The boom operator was a real pro, to Boz's amazement.

"Piece o' cake," Boz radioed. *Guess I still got it.*

The radio operator came back with, "Our boom operator Kai is sort of a legend around here, just like you are, sir. He's an old hand, in the Hawaiian guard. He told us he refueled dozens of Blackbirds as a young guy on Okinawa back in the day."

Boz threw an unseen salute in Kai's direction and decoupled.

He pulled up alongside the tanker, gave a thumbs-up, and hit the afterburners. Next stop Japan.

Midmorning on Okinawa, Boz touched down at Kadena Air Base. Same drill: gas up, take off, take on more fuel, and it was off to Kazakhstan.

I can't believe we're overflying China. I'm sure their newer SAMs could knock me down.

He had no choice, though. Every minute mattered.

"Aaron! You're at the airport already?" The old man's voice held a tinge of excitement as well as surprise.

"Hah," Aaron scoffed. "We got a problem. The border's sealed. I've surveyed the area twenty klicks on either side of the crossing. There's no way to get across on this bike. I could probably swim the river, but then I'm still hours away from the airport, on foot." He adjusted the sat phone against his ear. "Unless you got a new plan or can take out the two hundred soldiers crawling all over this place, I'm stuck."

FIFTY-FIVE

White House

"What the hell is an SR-71, and what's it doing over China?"

Steve Simpson felt his heart leap and his entire chest begin to tingle like he was about to have a panic attack. How could the president not know of the venerable old plane? He took a calming breath, pondering how he'd explain this one to the boss without triggering him further. "Sir, the SR-71 was an Air Force reconnaissance plane that we retired more than twenty years ago. It's the fastest plane on the planet. According to Pacific Command in Hawaii, Lockheed requested permission to perform a humanitarian mission—they're picking up a supply of the vaccine for this new virus—using one of these older planes. The air force is providing fuel to Lockheed and supporting the mission under disaster assistance authorities."

The puzzled expression remained on the president's face.

"According to Hawaii, the vaccine is in Kazakhstan. And—"

"Kazakhstan? Where's that? I thought it was in China."

"Sir, Kazakhstan is in Central Asia, not in China, but it borders China to the eas—"

"I know that, Simpson!" the president screamed. "I'm talking about the vaccine. Where's the vaccine?"

"Actually, sir, the Israelis are said to have smuggled the vaccine out of Russia into Kazakhstan."

"Goddamn it, Simpson. What have I told you about the Israelis? You can't trust them. And what has any of this got to do with Russia? And why are you doing this in the first place?"

"Mr. President. Look," Steve said with exaggerated patience, which the chief executive didn't seem to notice. "First, we aren't involved in this. Lockheed is a private company. And as far as Russia—"

"You aren't listening. This is about China, not Russia."

"Actually, sir, you're right. Your blockade is just now going into place. We were about to issue the ultimatum to Beijing when we learned about the SR-71. The Chinese picked up an overflight and protested. They're threatening to shoot down any other unknown aircraft that enters their airspace. And, sir, they claim the airspace around the Spratley Islands. That's where the blockade is going into effect," he checked his wristwatch, "right now."

Steve paused, unsure whether the president understood the problem. Seeing no glimmer of recognition, he continued. "Sir, if we try to enforce the blockade, we are likely to be met with force. And, that, Mr. President, could lead to an all-out war with China. You just can't do this blockade, sir."

"Well, who the hell authorized Hawaii to fly over China?"

Steve tried to remain calm. "Again, sir, the plane is private. It's flying to Kazakhstan to pick up a lifesaving vaccine. Remember, there's a possible outbreak of the new virus on one of the smaller Hawaiian Islands."

"Yes!" the president screamed. "By the Chinese! That's who released it."

"Yes, sir, it seems that way. But—"

"*No* buts, Simpson."

Steve's hands were shaking. He glared at the president. The president stared back and finally averted his gaze.

"Mr. President," Steve's voice quivered, "according to several intelligence reports, the North Koreans may have possession of the virus."

The president's brows drew together in a scowl.

"Sir, we don't know if the person who brought the virus to Hawaii—if that's what it really is—was Chinese, Korean, maybe Vietnamese, Japanese, or even American." Steve's voice rose through this speech. He maintained his glare at the president and finally shouted, "All we know is he's Asian. *Asian*, sir, not Chinese!"

The president opened his mouth, about to say something, but Steve barreled on, "And, sir, think of this! If *we* can get our hands on the vaccine and stop the virus from spreading, you'll be a fucking hero! Listen to me. The midterm elections are right around the corner. This would be the perfect October surprise. You could conceivably hold on to the House and win back the Senate. Mr. President! Please! Call off the goddamn blockade before it happens and let's keep our fingers crossed that Lockheed can get the vaccine!"

FIFTY-SIX

Southern Mongolia

"Where the fuck are you? I'm outta gas!" Boz screamed into his radio.

"About one hundred miles ahead and thirty-five thousand feet beneath you, sir. We're at forty thousand."

"Who the hell is this?"

"Captain John Briggs, Major Boswald, or should I call you Balls to the Wall, um, sir? I'm the pilot of the 135."

"Okay, I got you now. I'm coming in from behind. You ever tanked a Blackbird?"

"No, sir, but my dad did. He told me all about it, and about you. One reason I wanted to get in this business."

"Right. Just keep flying straight ahead at the same speed and deploy the boom."

"Roger that, sir."

Boz dove and lined the Blackbird up with the tanker.

Into the dead air, the captain said, "So, sir, the situation has changed. The White House is now involved. We are to follow you and tank you coming back out of Kazakhstan. We should be over eastern Kazakh by the time you take off. Also, they told us to be ready to light up our defensive suite just in case."

Boz nodded to himself. *Figures.*

"Looks like we're going to be heading west, like you, to Turkey. Got orders to stay away from China."

"Yeah," he said, "I don't want to go through that again. They lit me up."

The boom latched.

"Okay, looking good, Captain. Let's get this done."

FIFTY-SEVEN

Takoma Park, Maryland

The buzzing intensified. A bee divebombed her head, aiming at her face. It was trying to get in her mouth.

Chauncey's gentle grip on her bare shoulder woke her and Paula shook off the nightmare. Her cell phone buzzed again and she grabbed it from the nightstand. "Hello?" she mumbled and tried to quietly clear her throat.

"Paula." The deep scratchy voice could only be Ari Schweitzman. "I'm sorry to wake you, but this is urgent."

Paula sat up, fully awake. *How does he know my number? Oh yeah, right. Mossad.* "Yes?"

"I'm afraid I have some bad news. It seems our agent is unable to cross the border from Russia to Kazakhstan. He can't get to the Kostanay Airport."

"Oh no," Paula moaned. She looked at the digital clock radio on her nightstand. It was approaching midnight in DC. That was when the SR-71 was supposed to land in Kazakhstan. "What are we going to do?"

"Well, I have an idea, a plan B, but I'm not sure it will work."

Heck, none of this was guaranteed to work. "What is it?"

"I have positioned my agent with the vaccine to the north of

Kostanay Airport where there is an old two-thousand-meter airstrip. It's not in very good shape." He paused for a split second. "But, well, what is worse is the airfield is in Russia. Would your people land there and pick up the vaccine? I fear it is our only hope."

Paula was stunned. *He wants us to land in Russia? And then get out of there without getting arrested or shot down by a surface-to-air missile? That's the craziest thing I've ever heard.*

"It is the best I can arrange under the circumstances," the deep voice continued. "We are running out of time for the vaccine to remain viable. Of course, Russian air defense might be a problem, and border forces are swarming the area. It would be quite risky. But we are out of options . . . and time."

I can't ask Rich Kelly to do this. She shook her head. *But what choice do we have?* She thought for only a few seconds. "Okay, I'll tell Lockheed. Have your agent standing by in case they agree to land there. If not, well, at least we tried."

The voice on the other end shouted, "Trying is not enough! We must succeed! We are so close! You must convince them! It is the only way! We must rescue Aaron! I mean, the world." The older man coughed as if he was seeking to compose himself. The next time he spoke, his voice had regained its moderate tone. "Excuse me, Paula, but please try to convince them. We simply must get the vaccine before it is too late. I understand your country may already be at risk from exposure."

Paula wrinkled her nose. *At risk? What's he talking about?* She reassured him she'd do her best and clicked off. She searched for Rich Kelly's cell number and placed the call.

"Kelly."

"Sir, I'm sorry to call so late, but it's urgent."

"No problem. Boswald should be landing soon. He had a scare over China but made it okay. Said he's glad he's not going back that way. It surprises the hell out of me, but this crazy plan of yours just might work."

"Yes, sir. That's great, but we have a new problem. The vaccine is still in Russia."

"What? What the hell happened? That blows the plan to smithereens! Boz can't sit on the ground in Kazakhstan. He'll get stuck there. And the tanker can't wait forever."

Paula explained the problem.

"Christ. I don't know, Paula, that's asking an awful lot of Boz. And I really don't want to lose my plane."

"I understand completely, sir, but I have to ask." She paused and took a deep breath. "It's the only way. But you're right. The risk is enormous. And who knows if the vaccine is even any good at this point. The Israelis will just have to get their agent out of Russia on their own. But, listen, Mr. Kelly. I want to thank you for what you've done. I mean, this has been insane, and you've taken my word for it. Sent your last Blackbird halfway around the world on a wild goose chase. I know you didn't have to do that. And I really appreciate your trying."

"Well, Paula, I've known you and your former boss a long time. I figure if the two of you are behind this, as crazy as it sounds it must be legit. Tell you what, I'll radio Boswald and let him make the decision. Like you say, it might be our only way to save the world from the terrorists. Losing my SR-71, well, I guess it would be worth the risk."

"But what about your pilot?"

"Oh hell, Boswald can take care of himself. If you're right about the location of the airstrip, he'd only be in Russia for a couple minutes, tops. Even if their air defense missiles got off a lucky shot, he'll be across the border when he punches out of the cockpit."

"Gee, sir. I can't believe you're agreeing to try," Paula said, looking down and grabbing Chauncey's hand that was resting on her waist. She gave it a squeeze. "I'll let the air force know the change of plan. It might pucker them up, but at least they'll know to have their forces on alert."

FIFTY-EIGHT

Chelyabinsk Oblast, Russia

He crouched behind a handful of waist-high steel drums with his black jacket zipped up and his ski cap pulled down covering as much skin as possible to ward off the freezing temperature. A cold gust of wind made him shiver. Across the runway, smoke was billowing from the chimney of what had to be the airfield manager's office. *Someone must be in there.*

"Aaron, no matter how things turn out, I want you to know how much I appreciate your willingness to take on this incredibly hazardous and complex mission. I know you will never forgive me for the girl's death," his mentor's voiced droned on, "even though I've told you many times it wasn't our fault. The poor thing must have jumped. I had no idea she loved you that much. You are a son to me. I would never—"

"Enough bullshit. Is the transport coming or not?" Aaron was hiding as well as he could behind a rusted-out Quonset hut beside the tiny Russian airstrip. There was no tower. In fact, he couldn't see any sign of instrumentation for guiding planes. The runway was pockmarked, but he knew American C-17s could land almost anywhere.

"The short answer is, I don't know. If he is coming, it will be soon. Are you still at the airfield?"

Two aging AN-2 turboprop aircraft and a small crop duster were tied down on concrete pads adjacent to the so-called runway. He might be able to steal a plane, but then what? "Yes, but we're running out of time. The vaccine won't last much longer." Aaron's head was on a swivel checking all around for any sign of police, soldiers, border patrol. None in sight.

He looked to the east. A glint of sunlight reflected off of an aircraft approaching at low altitude, nearly skimming the treetops, as it hurtled in his direction. He muttered, "That's not a transport, must be a Russian fighter. I've got to find a better spot to hide."

"A plane? Do you see a plane?"

Aaron ended the call and stood, ready to dash to the storage shed across the way. But it was too late. The plane was landing.

The pilot's nose gear hit the edge of the poorly paved surface and screamed down the runway. He popped a chute, and the bird started to slow down.

What the hell? That looks like that old American spy plane. Aaron checked the tail as it slowed down and saw LOCKHEED on it. He made a beeline for the runway.

The plane reached the end of the paved surface and nimbly turned around. It jettisoned the chute and started back down the runway as if it was going to take off again. Aaron sprinted onto the bumpy surface waving his arms.

The aircraft jerked to a halt and the canopy popped open. The pilot ripped off his oxygen mask. "If you're the Israeli, get your ass in this plane! If not, I'm outta here!"

Aaron threw him a thumbs-up and leaped, just able to grasp the wingtip. It was hotter than hell even in the frigid air. He pulled himself onto the surface and scampered to the airplane's tandem cockpit. "I don't believe it!" he gasped. "Where'd you get this old bucket of bolts, a museum?"

"Don't knock it, pardner. It's the only bird that has a chance of saving our asses. Get yourself strapped in. But I gotta tell you, I'm not sure you're gonna make it with that beard. The oxygen mask won't fit."

Aaron jumped in the open seat, nearly stepping in an ice bucket. He flicked open his switchblade.

The pilot saw the knife and pulled out a pistol. He aimed it over his shoulder. "I don't know what your game is, dude, but drop the knife or you're a fuckin' dead man."

Aaron grabbed his beard and started hacking it off in huge clumps, his eyes never leaving the pilot's. "How'd you find this place? And what's with the ice bucket, you got champagne somewhere?" He winked.

The pilot grinned. "Ice is for the vaccine. Best we could do under the circumstances. Not sure it will help, but it sure as hell can't hurt. Air Force gave me the coordinates. . . . Piece o' cake. Can't believe Russian air defense didn't spot me. The Chinese sure as hell did."

Aaron smiled and scraped off more of his beard.

Several shots cracked the air. Aaron dropped the knife and returned fire with his pistol, causing the Russians emerging from the field office to scamper for cover. He pulled on his oxygen mask even though clumps of dark whiskers still stuck out. "Just get us out of here!"

The pilot lowered the canopy and punched the throttle. The Blackbird sprang to life and roared down the choppy runway. After takeoff, he banked gently to the right and exited Russian airspace as rapidly as possible.

FIFTY-NINE

Kazakhstan

"Okay, Major, you're good to go. Or should I call you 'Balls to the Wall'?"

Boz chuckled. "Boz is fine, Captain. Thanks for the gas. And thanks for cranking up your wall of sound or whatever caused the Russians' radar to go haywire."

"Pleasure's all ours, sir. Luckily, Russian air defense isn't very robust here. They redeployed most of their assets to the north once Finland joined NATO."

Always better to be lucky than good. Boz smiled.

"Sir, I got one late-breaking change for you. INDOPACOM says you need to fly to Hawaii instead of DC."

"Hawaii? What the hell. Why? That makes no sense." The tanker nozzle had disengaged and Boz was about to blast out of the neighborhood. "Unless you're providing cover, the Chinese are gonna shoot my ass out of the sky."

"Sorry, sir. No can do. I got orders to head to Incirlik in Turkey. Got just enough fuel myself to get there. No way I can make it back to Japan. You're on your own."

"Well, fuck 'em. They can't order me to do anything."

"Yes, sir. The problem is, there's been an outbreak of the virus in Hawaii. They need the vaccine there as fast as possible. I guess there's a couple of victims and everyone's panicked the virus could escape and kill us all." The captain paused, letting that sink in. "They've suggested you overfly Mongolia. Spend as little time over China as possible."

"Ah, shit. Yeah, I guess Mongolia makes sense. But it won't work. The Chinese will be tracking me all the way and could launch as soon as I cross into their airspace."

"Uh, yes, sir. You're probably right." The air went silent.

Boz gritted his teeth. This bird was fast, but not as fast as Chinese missiles.

"Sir, they've arranged a tanker to meet you over the Sea of Japan, once you clear Chinese airspace. They're also sending a tanker out of Hawaii to meet you on the way in to make sure you got enough fuel. They want you to land on the island of Kauai at the navy base. They'll give you more info when you tank in Japan."

"Yeah, okay." Boz whistled under his breath. "I'm getting too old for this shit."

"And, sir? Good luck. The world's counting on you."

"Thanks. Adios, amigo.

"*Vaya con Dios*, Boz."

"Okay, dude," Boz spoke to his passenger. "Better hold on tight, it's gonna be a bumpy ride. What's your name, anyhow? I'm Boz."

Aaron paused for a second. "Call me Jake, Boz."

"Okay, what gives? You're supposed to be Israeli, but you sure sound like a Yank."

"It's a long story."

"Well, we got a couple hours ahead of us, so start spewing."

SIXTY

Takoma Park, Maryland

Paula had just fallen back to sleep when her phone buzzed her awake. "Hello?" she answered sleepily.

"Paula, it's Dan Cooper. I'm sorry to wake you. I know it's after one a.m. in DC, but I thought you should know, we've got the package and we're heading to Hawaii."

"Hawaii? What? Why? We need to get it to DC, to Detrick, sir."

"I don't suppose you have a secure phone, do you?"

"No, sir, I'm at home. Last I heard the vaccine was in Russia."

"I can't comment on any of that on an open line. What I can say, if you'll keep it to yourself, is we believe there is an outbreak of the virus on Niihau."

"Niihau? I'm sorry, sir, but that can't be. Niihau is cut off from the rest of the world. Outsiders can't visit, it's a private island. It's the last place on earth where Native Hawaiian culture, language, and customs are observed. How would they have been exposed?"

"Again, this is sensitive, but we're told an Asian man swam onto the island and infected one of the locals. Then the Asian man died of extreme flu-like symptoms. Now the Native Hawaiian who found him is in a very bad way. And he, in turn, infected his wife. She's the one who got in touch with the folks on Kauai. The state is planning to put a hazmat unit on the island, but without the vaccine that would only increase the risk of spreading the virus. The presi— . . . um . . . DC made the decision to send the plane to Hawaii instead of Detrick to try to stop the spread. Problem is, we're out of time. We might get to Hawaii in time, but no way we can then send it on to DC before it goes inert. We've got just enough fuel in theater for the bird to get here."

Paula pressed her fingers to the bridge of her nose. "Well, Admiral, I guess stopping an outbreak on Niihau makes the most sense at this point."

Admiral Cooper said, "We have to hope this is the only outbreak, or we get lucky and the vaccine lasts longer than a day."

"Yep. If there's any left over and it's still usable, I'd send it over to Manoa, on Oahu. UH, the University of Hawaii, does a lot of work on infectious diseases. They also do vaccine research. I mean, their scientists are nowhere as prepared or well trained as Fort Detrick's, but if anybody on Hawaii could figure out the chemical compound, it's probably them. I can give you the dean's number if you want to contact him."

"Sounds like a plan. A Hail Mary pass for sure, but this whole thing has been one all along and we've got this far. So long as Lockheed's pilot can evade Chinese air defenses, we're still in the ball game. Thanks for the tip on UH. I'll give them a call."

SIXTY-ONE

Mongolian Border

"Okay, Jake, hold on to your socks! We're entering Chinese airspace and they've already lit us up!" Boz screamed into the radio headset.

The Blackbird was at eighty thousand feet when his controls indicated a surface-to-air missile was headed their way. He upped his speed to Mach 3, but the SAM was closing fast.

He yanked back on the stick and pushed the Blackbird toward heaven. The missile kept closing. The altimeter hit 85, 87, 89. The missile was about to impact.

"It's been nice knowing ya, Jake, see you on the other side." Boz pushed his speed to Mach 3.3 and offered a silent prayer.

A low moan came over the headset. Jake must have been struggling to get enough oxygen out of that ill-fitting mask and was losing consciousness. The HQ 9 missile couldn't have been more than a hundred meters out when Boz heard an unmistakable pop from the automatic countermeasures dispenser deploying flares. He tilted the nose slightly downward and watched as the missile flew over him and locked onto one of the flares.

"Well, I'll be damned. The effing thing worked. We're golden, Jake." He peered over his shoulder and saw Jake slumped in his seat.

"Ah, shit. I sure hope ya just fainted. You should be okay in a couple minutes." Just then his instruments blared, indicating he'd been acquired by Russian air defense radars.

"Ah, shit. We must be over Russia now. They got S-400 missiles near Vladivostok and we're about to fly right overhead." He turned to a more southerly heading and eased the nose of the aircraft back up. "But it's either that or North Korea." He took a quick glance across the crowded control panel before him. "If we can hold 'em off for another three minutes, we'll be safe. Or maybe this bird's got some other new tricks to stop them?"

They rocketed toward the heavens. "Yee haw!" Boz screamed. At ninety thousand feet they hit Mach 3.4 and overflew Vladivostok out to the Sea of Japan.

Over Hokkaido Island, at the north end of Japan, the tanker contacted him: "Sir, this is Captain McCloud, we're running low on your fuel. I got about a half tank for you is all. Another bird will meet you about a thousand miles off of Hawaii and direct you where to land. Man, that must've been some flying you did!"

"Dude, that was better than riding forty-foot waves at Maverick's. Un-fucking-believable! Haven't heard a peep from my passenger, though. He conked out over China. Thanks for the gas, Captain." Boz hit the afterburners and blasted out of Asia.

SIXTY-TWO

South Pacific

"How ya doing, Jake? You still with me?"

"I'm okay. My head hurts. I think I was in and out of consciousness. It was like I couldn't catch my breath. Maybe over China. I thought I heard you saying something about Russia?"

"You bet. All that. Well, we're cleared to land at the navy's Pacific Missile Range on Kauai, but we're just about out of Schlitz."

"What?"

"Old timer's expression, dude. We tanked somewhere near Midway Island, but they didn't have much gas. Looks like we just about drained the supply of JP-7 from the Eastern Hemisphere. I figure we'll land on fumes, maybe have to coast in, which could be real fun. It'll be like sliding into home with Johnny Bench blocking the plate."

"Who?"

"Ah, never mind. Just hang on tight."

Aaron could feel the plane descending rapidly. *Holy shit. This is nuts.* He looked out the cockpit, but all he could see was dark water getting closer and closer.

"Here we go, dude. It's gonna get bumpy!" Boz hollered.

Bam! The Blackbird hit the ground at what had to be over four hundred kilometers per hour! Jake felt the initial crash and then a secondary crash as if the landing gear collapsed, and the belly of the aircraft bounced along the runway. In a few brief moments, they came to a skidding stop and the aircraft spun sideways.

"Ah, shit. That'll do it for this bird. But she did the mission. Aloha, Jake, we be in Hawaii." Boz sounded exhilarated, as if he had just stepped off a roller coaster.

Aaron felt as if his stomach had collided with his esophagus. He figured he'd shrunk about two inches with all of his vertebrae smashed together. *Jesus Christ. But we're here.* He loosened his grip on the cockpit's side panels.

The canopy flipped open as the navy base fire trucks arrived on the scene. They sprayed fire suppression foam on the underside of the plane where it rested on the runway. Boz popped out of the cockpit. He looked at Aaron. "That was an E-ticket ride if I ever had one. Too bad we couldn't stick the landing. I did the best I could. But, hey, we're alive."

"That was some flying, Boz," Aaron said, shaking his head in amazement. "I mean, even if I missed half of it, you sure know how to handle this baby."

"Oh, yeah. I love this shit. Nowadays all I get to fly is a tiny Cessna turbo. This sucker's a Ferrari or maybe one of those rocket cars out on the Bonneville Salt Flats. Rich ain't gonna be too happy about what I did to her. But knowing him and his guys at Skunk Works, they'll get her flying again at some point. They'll probably sail her back to Palmdale to get fixed up because she won't be flying anywhere anytime soon."

Navy sailors wheeled an aircraft maintenance ladder up to the plane. Boswald climbed down. A navy captain approached the plane and called out, "You Major Boswald, sir?"

"Well, I was about twenty years ago. Call me Boz."

"Yes, sir. I'm Skip Wilton, base commander. Have you got the vaccine?"

Boswald pointed to Aaron. "Talk to Jake. It's his."

The captain had a quizzical look on his face as he studied Aaron, taking in his disheveled appearance. Patches of dark whiskers stuck out from his chin and he was sure bright red scratches covered his cheeks. He had on his black leather jacket and jeans and was probably not who the captain was expecting to see climbing out of the backseat of the old recon plane.

"I've got six vials on ice," Aaron said, raising the ice bucket. "Well, what little ice that's left." He joggled the bucket and ice water sloshed around inside. "I was supposed to get this to DC before it's dead. No way we're gonna be able to do that now," he said, motioning toward the wrecked SR-71.

"Ah, yes, sir." Commander Wilton nodded. "We've had a virus outbreak on the island of Niihau. A Chinese man came ashore and infected two of the residents. We've got a hazmat unit on that helo over there." He pointed to a helicopter parked on the side of the runway about a hundred feet away. Its rotor was already turning. "They'll take it to the victims on Niihau." He pointed to another navy helo about fifty feet beyond that one. "We'll take the remaining vials over to Oahu, to the university, for them to study. They've got a team standing by tonight to identify the vaccine's components."

Aaron, still holding onto the ice bucket, looked at both helicopters. He reached into the cold water and pulled out the six lifesaving vials. He offered four to the commander. "Here. You can have these for research. I'll take these two out to the victims. No reason to expose a hazmat team."

Commander Wilton reached out both hands, making a basket, and accepted the four vials. He turned to his aide and said, "Get these on ice ASAP." He turned his attention back to Aaron. "What do you mean? You're keeping the others? How does that work?"

"I'm vaccinated. I jabbed myself with the vaccine at the lab in Russia. So I'm the only one who can safely go out to the island to try to save those people. Plus, I can fend off the attacker if he's still there. It's got to be Kim. He's not Chinese. He's a North Korean agent who stole the virus from the Russians. I can make sure the disease doesn't spread. Just put me on the chopper and I'll rappel down to the victims. You don't even have to land."

"But how will you get back?"

"Don't worry about me. I'll be fine." He started walking toward the helicopter where the hazmat team waited. "Get them off the bird, and make sure you've got a rope for me to climb down. Is there a radio on that island so I can send word back when I've inoculated the victims?" His satellite phone still nestled in his jacket, but he wasn't about to let the Americans know that.

"Affirmative, sir. But my orders are to send the hazmat team. I can't let you go out there."

Aaron stopped, turned to the navy officer, and pierced him with a steely gaze. "Listen, Captain. I've just flown halfway around the world after spending all night being chased by the Russian military and then border patrol. I lost a colleague. That was after I broke into the Russian lab and stole this vaccine. Oh yeah, right before I blew up their effing facility. I don't give a shit about your orders. Now get the hazmat team off the goddamn bird, give me a couple hypodermic needles, and get me to that island!"

Boswald let out a war whoop and laughed. "If I were you, Cap'n, I'd take him up on his offer. He's obviously crazy or he wouldn't have gone through all that." Boswald looked down at his watch. "And if what he says about the vaccine is right, you can't waste any more time worrying about military protocol. That shit's about to turn rancid or something. This be your last chance, dude. Don't fuck it up."

The captain shook his head and, following Aaron to the helicopter, he radioed the pilot and gave the new orders. "That's what I said, rope suspension, drop him, and return to base."

Aaron boarded the chopper and they took off for the eight-minute flight to Niihau. Once over the verdant island, he spotted lights from a single-story building. He grabbed the rope and was lowered to the ground.

He hit the surface, gave a thumbs-up to the pilot, and stood there for a moment. *This is for you, Melissa.*

He could hear coughing coming from inside the small cottage. He knocked on the door and, not waiting, entered. An older woman was lying on a couch. She looked in a bad way. He could tell she was struggling to breathe. As he approached, a horrified look appeared on her face.

"Don't worry, ma'am. I'm here to give you a vaccine for the disease. Can you tell me where your husband is?"

She pointed toward a doorway on the other side of the room. Aaron nodded. He pulled out a vial of vaccine, loaded the needle, and gently administered the shot. He stroked her arm softly where he'd made the injection and smiled down into her pained face. "This is supposed to fix you right up, ma'am, although it might take a day or two before you really feel better."

She closed her eyes and seemed to relax a little.

"I'll be right back. Sit tight."

He walked into the bedroom. An old man was lying still on the bed. Aaron rushed over and felt for a pulse. The Native Hawaiian man was still alive, but his pulse was very weak. Aaron laid a hand over the man's mouth. A tiny amount of air was being exhaled. He pulled out the second vial and gave this victim the dose. *We'll see if this works. This guy doesn't look like he'll make it.*

He walked back into the main room. The woman was watching him. She pointed out where the radio sat on a side table in the rudimentary kitchen area. He dialed up Kauai and informed them that both people were alive, but that the man was in very bad shape. He signed off saying he'd radio again in the morning.

He tried to get the woman to tell him where Kim was, but all she could muster was "beach." He smiled and told her to try to sleep. With any luck, she would feel better in the morning.

Aaron walked into the bathroom and caught sight of his face in the mirror. *Jesus, it's a wonder she didn't have a heart attack. I look like the Wolfman.* He spotted a razor on the sink and helped himself to a shave. Next he headed outside, but it was way too dark to find Kim. A hammock was hanging between two palm trees and he slid into it.

Just before dawn, he awoke to the crowing of roosters. He spun out of the hammock and headed off to find the North Korean. The first thing he spotted was the mini submarine that had washed onto the beach. He pulled it farther up onto the sand, aimed its solar panels toward the morning sun, and continued his search for Kim. He found the body about a hundred meters from the low tide mark on a trail he suspected led to the village. He stood a handful of meters back and observed the corpse for a moment, then, giving the body a wide berth, he churned up the sandy trail.

Back at the village, he knocked on the older couple's door.

"Come in," a weak voice called out.

Aaron opened the door and smiled. The woman was propped up on one elbow. "How are you feeling?" he asked.

She tried to smile and flopped her head from side to side.

He nodded. "Well, I think you should lie back down and rest. You're looking a lot better than last night."

"Husband?"

Tears were welling in her eyes. He turned to the bedroom, expecting the worst.

He knocked lightly on the doorjamb. The man's head moved a little at the sound. Aaron went over and felt his pulse. It was stronger. The man's breathing was still weak, but much better than it had been the night before.

Aaron brought both of them a glass of water, helping each in turn to sit up and drink. The man was extremely weak, but improving. The woman wanted to get up, but Aaron insisted she stay on the couch. He radioed Kauai their progress and then scrambled some eggs on a two-burner cooktop. He was able to get both patients to eat a little.

In a nearby shed he found a gas can, matches, and a shovel and headed to the beach.

Kim's body was beginning to deteriorate. Aaron wrapped large leaves around the ankles and dragged it off the beach. He dug a hole, rolled the body in, soaked it in gasoline, and cremated the corpse. He figured that was the best way to ensure the virus couldn't escape. He filled the hole and stuck in the shovel as a makeshift headstone to alert the community of where the remains were buried.

It was already afternoon by the time he got back to the village. When he knocked on the door and started to push it ajar, he was surprised the woman opened it. He could tell she was still weak by the way she clung to the doorknob. He helped her back to the couch. He cooked another batch of scrambled eggs and made her and her husband eat. The man was starting to look a little better, but still struggling. After feeding them and eating himself, Aaron sat outside in the warm sun. It was only then that he decided to call the old man.

"I have tended to the two victims and destroyed the body of the terrorist. The Americans are studying the remaining vials of vaccine. The attacker, a North Korean named Kim whom I met in Russia, arrived on the island in a battery-powered mini sub. I'm now recharging it by solar panels. As soon as the couple here is okay, I will sail the sub off the island on a northwest heading. I will remain close to the surface and will turn on the sat phone every six hours so you can track my location. Send a ship to pick me up before I die of thirst." Aaron coldly hammered out the details of his update and his plan.

"That is wonderful news, my son. We were aware that you made it to safety in America. But are you certain that the submarine is the best extraction plan? Return to Kauai. The Americans will fly you home."

"Have you lost your mind?" Aaron's lip curled in a sneer he knew the old man couldn't see but was sure to hear. "I can't go to an American airport or military base. I'm a wanted man. Because of you. Or have you forgotten about my last visit to Washington?"

"Of course I haven't. Perhaps you are right. We have commercial vessels in the Pacific. I will redirect one to your location in twelve hours. Good luck. I will see you when you get home."

"Well, you can forget about that. I'm not coming back. I told you before, I refuse to do your killing. Just get me on a ship." He switched off the phone and walked back inside.

Aaron found a pot of leftover soup in the refrigerator and put it on the stove to simmer. He could hear the woman speaking a strange language in the bedroom. He peeked his head in. She was sitting on the bed holding the old man's hand. The husband was awake. They both looked up to see him in the doorway. "I think you are well enough for me to leave. If it's okay with you, I am going to take this canteen I found in your shed, and I took the liberty of grabbing a loaf of your bread. I have a long journey."

"Take what you need," the woman said. "You saved our lives. We will never forget you. But how will you get off the island?"

"Don't worry about me. I have a ride." He smiled, waved, and left the house.

SIXTY-THREE

Washington, DC

"I told you, Charley. You can't keep a secret in this town." Elise Warnke stood in front of the majority leader holding up the front page of the *Washington Examiner*. The photo above the fold showed Senator Lackland lying in bed with an oxygen tube in his nose and an IV in his arm. He had a sickly gray visage and looked near death. In her other hand she held a cup of coffee, an attempt to jolt herself awake. It was only seven a.m., the earliest she could ever remember being in the leader's office in the Capitol.

"Damn it, Elise, why did Beverly Lackland think she needed to give a press conference and challenge them to find out the truth about Harry?"

Elise had to suppress a gasp. "Charley, we're the ones who challenged the press," she snapped. "We set her up. The press was hounding her. What was the poor woman supposed to do?"

"I suppose. But we're in a world of hurt now. No way the press'll believe we didn't know what was going on. Shoot. Less than a week until the election and this has to happen."

"That's right." She dropped the newspaper on his desk and cupped her mug. "My staff tells me the Republicans are already buying up every available thirty-second TV spot they can get. They're flooding all the radio stations in New Hampshire, Iowa, Georgia, and even Pennsylvania, where Jimmy Capton said we're up by twenty points. I don't know what to tell you, Charley." *But don't think I didn't warn you. You and Rostow, so confident you could keep the lid on this.*

"I guess the only thing we can do now is claim that, at the request of Beverly, we stayed quiet and were hoping that—as she keeps claiming—he'd make a full recovery." Charley looked up at her for support.

Elise shook her head. "I guess. But it's not likely to work. The article says an unnamed source at Walter Reed admitted that Lackland isn't likely to recover any of his faculties. And their editorial demands that Lackland step down immediately."

Charley seemed to be shrinking behind his desk.

"For all practical purposes," she continued, "by the time Virginia appoints a replacement, we'll be out of session. You're leader until January and longer, depending on what happens in the races. But if the election goes south, well, not much we can do. Guess we just keep our fingers crossed that this October surprise is too late to affect the elections. But if you ask me, I think this will sink us."

SIXTY-FOUR

White House

"Mr. President, are you ready?" Steve Simpson knew his voice sounded upbeat for the first time in weeks.

President Parker, seated behind the Resolute Desk, wore a dark, sharply tailored suit, crisp white shirt, and red, white, and blue striped tie. The American flag was prominently displayed in the background. He looked into the mirror his makeup man had given him. He gave the mirror his familiar smug smile and nodded at his reflection. He handed it back, dismissed the assistant, and looked over at his chief of staff. "I'm ready."

"Very good. The cameras will start rolling when you give a thumbs-up. The teleprompter script large enough for you?"

Parker nodded again. He sat up straight in his chair and gave the thumbs-up. After counting to five under his breath, he began to speak.

"Good evening, my fellow Americans. In recent weeks our nation and the nations of our allies have been threatened by a bloodthirsty group of terrorists who sought to destroy mankind. You have all seen the news reports of a tiny hamlet in Central Asia being devastated by the release of a new, engineered coronavirus that causes a disease so deadly it cripples and kills its victims in a matter of hours.

"My administration has focused on rooting out these despicable terrorists and destroying their deadly bioweapon. That's right, it is a bioweapon. This disease is a man-made concoction designed to kill humans. When we first learned of the threat, I vowed that no pandemic would shut down our economy. They wouldn't force you, the American people, to retreat once again behind your closed doors.

"I am pleased to tell you that tonight the threat has been abated. The country—in fact, the world—is once again safe from this deadly weapon.

"Acting in concert with our allies and in partnership with American industry, our military has destroyed the source of the virus. And tonight, as we speak, our scientists are working overtime analyzing a lifesaving vaccine that can defeat this virus should it ever reappear.

"Many details of our successful mission must remain classified to protect national security. Rest assured that our nation, you, your children, and neighbors, are safe. Let me repeat. The terrorists have failed. The virus is no longer a threat to this or any other country. So, please, go to your places of worship, to the movie theaters, to restaurants, to ball games, and to our great national parks knowing that you are not threatened.

"As we approach the midterm congressional elections, I ask only one thing of you. Give me partners in the House and Senate who will work with me, on your behalf, to continue to serve you. I urge you to exercise your right to vote next Tuesday and help me preserve our democracy.

"God bless our men and women in uniform, and God bless the United States of America. Good night."

The klieg lights clicked off, signaling that filming had ended.

Steve Simpson applauded and was joined by the half dozen technical assistants in the room. "That was terrific, Mr. President. Our candidates are already at work making campaign ads using this footage. They will remind voters of your success and your request that they vote for our guys and gals. With any luck our fellow Americans will be rushing out to vote Republican next Tuesday."

"That's great, Steve. Does this mean we can finally start work on the golf course?"

SIXTY-FIVE

Wednesday, the day after the election
Dirksen Senate Office Building

Paula wrapped the framed photo of her family in bubble wrap and placed it in the cardboard box on top of her desk. Someone knocked on the open door, startling her.

"Got a minute?" *Roll Call* reporter Harris Ward stood in the doorway wearing an appropriate Harris Tweed sport coat, crewneck sweater, and faded blue jeans. His hair was hanging down on his forehead and he pushed it back. He must have known that he'd surprised her. He added, "There wasn't anyone in the front office and the door was unlocked." He paused for a second. "I see you're packing already."

Paula smiled. "Yeah, under any circumstance I'll be moving out. We lost the Senate, so I'll be moving to the minority office. That is, if I stay."

Harris let out a surprised laugh. "You just got back! You can't really be thinking about leaving?"

Paula scrunched up her face and tilted her head to the side. "Oh, Harris, I don't know. Well, first of all, with Lackland's resignation last week, I lost my sponsor. Pat Sistrunk hired me, and he's clearly out now."

"Yeah, we're losing our hundred and first senator." He winked at her.

"You're terrible. Pat's not a bad guy. He means well. And, with what happened to Chairman Lackland and the coverup, what choice did he have? And I don't know if Senator Boyer wants to keep me anyway. Whatever." She shrugged. "Besides, it doesn't look like she'll remain ranking Democrat on the subcommittee."

"Yeah, I heard that. Lon Ellers is senior. He's told anyone who'll listen he's replacing Lackland. He's also told me privately that he'll bump Boyer. He never forgave Lackland for giving her Defense. It almost sounded like he was glad about what happened to Chairman Lackland." He scowled.

Paula nodded. "I can believe that. Seems like we're a little short of collegiality these days. Anyway, even if I can stay, I'm not sure I will. I mean, Chauncey wants to go back to Hawaii. He says he's a fish out of water here. And he thinks the Old Dominion and even Maryland are still not ready to accept mixed-race families. I hate to say it, but he may be right. And, well, you know, Harris, things have really changed around here. I mean, Mitsunaga's gone, of course. Jackson's gone, now Lackland. The level of trust that the old bulls had in one another, well, that seems to be gone too. It's like the mood is always negative. Ugh." She pressed her fingertips against her eyes and growled under her breath.

"Everyone wants to fight about the tiniest things!" she stormed on, as if she had to convince herself it'd be worth it to leave. "And it's on both sides. Not just Republicans like George, who constantly try to throw a monkey wrench into the works. From what I see, my chairman, Boyer, is getting a little better at working with the other side. But even so, I think her gut reaction is always that the other party is trying to screw with us." Paula frowned. "You know, I love this place, but, well, maybe I love what I remember about it." A tired smile crept on her face. "Anyhoo. What brings you here the day after an election, when nothing is happening?"

"I'm chasing down a crazy rumor that involves you," he said pointblank.

"Me?" Paula collapsed in her chair, wrinkling her forehead anxiously.

Harris stood there for a moment smiling. "You know, I can't really believe I'm actually asking this."

Paula leaned forward with a very quizzical expression. "Okay." She waited. "And?"

Harris held up his hands. "Alright. It's crazy, but I heard from a very reliable source who says he got it from someone in the Pentagon that you," he pointed at her with both index fingers, "were behind this rescue mission that saved the people on that island in Hawaii. Now I know that doesn't make any sense at all. I mean, yeah, you worked for Senator Mitsunaga, and you've lived in Hawaii, but so what? How could you be behind this? Anyway, I promised the guy I'd check it out. So disabuse me of this fantasy."

Paula felt her cheeks pale. Her eyes opened wide. "Harris, you can't print that."

"Of course not," he scoffed, then stopped. "Wait. You are going to deny it, aren't you?"

"Well," Paula leaned back and slid a little lower in her chair. "Just don't print the story, okay? Please."

"But how could you be responsible? The White House is claiming credit. And I hear it was a Lockheed plane. What's your connection?"

Paula tried to formulate her thoughts. "That's all correct."

"But?" Harris stepped a little closer.

"Well, some of it is sensitive, probably classified, so I can't share the details."

"Okay. . . . Tell me what you can."

"Harris, listen, I will only tell you the story if you promise not to print it." She gave him a piercing look, but he didn't respond. "Look at it from my point of view. Like you said, President Parker is out there claiming complete responsibility for the rescue. He's saying he saved the world and won the election for the GOP. Do you realize what trouble I'd be in—with both parties—if you write that I was involved? Even if it were true. Heck, I'd be out of a job here and in Hawaii too. Chauncey and I and the boys might not even be safe." She paused, hoping he'd respond, but he didn't. "Okay, I mean it. If you want the story, you have to promise this is off the record and you won't print it. You won't mention me or the committee or the Senate or Mitsunaga or anyone else connected to me. Agreed?"

Harris plopped down in the chair in front of Paula's desk. "Alright. I promise I won't make any reference to you or the Senate, et cetera, but the story needs to be told. Just leave out anything you think would be classified of course. I don't want to be accused of leaking secrets."

Paula got up and closed both doors. She came back and sat down in the chair next to Harris.

Harris pulled his reporter's notebook out of his jacket pocket and Paula began. "I got a call from Senator Mitsunaga asking me to meet with an Israeli."

"That's unbelievable. I mean, it's really hard to believe, but it all tracks with what I've been hearing. Amazing." Harris had scribbled as fast as he could to get the whole scoop.

"Yeah, and now you should understand why I'm asking you to kill the story."

He nodded and stood up. Stuffing his notebook in his jacket pocket, he thanked her. He turned to leave but spun back around. "You know, if this were to get out, it would be you that they'd be calling the hundred and first senator." He winked and walked out of her office.

EPILOGUE

I
January
Pearl Harbor, Hawaii

Paula stepped out of the bright sunshine into the dimly lit all hands club at Joint Base Pearl Harbor. After a couple seconds, her eyes adjusted and she did a quick scan around the joint. *Oh, yeah, I've been here before. But it's been a while.* It would take a while longer for her body temperature to acclimate to the air force's arctic air-conditioning.

The motif was tiki bar, a tad out of date and more than a little culturally inappropriate. But the place was packed for *pau hana.* Sitting alone at a small table in the corner was a youngish woman with fiery red curls in a green sundress. *That's got to be her.* She walked up and smiled. "Amy?"

"That's me." The redheaded woman looked up and smiled. "You must be Paula. Fred told me you were beautiful. Boy, he wasn't lying." She motioned to a chair. "Have a seat."

Paula felt herself flush and sat down. "He didn't tell me how cute you were. I love the red hair." Paula eased into the worn leather club chair. "So, how well do you know Fred?"

Amy flinched a tad. She leaned closer to Paula. "You might not believe this, but he literally saved my life." She glanced around the bar.

"I'm not allowed to talk about it. It's part of a deal I signed with, um, headquarters that kept me out of Leavenworth." She winked. "Funny, you know, in my business, I used to work at, um, Belvoir, right?"

Paula nodded. "Fred didn't go into the details, but yeah, he told me a little about the trouble you got in."

"Hah. Trouble with a capital T. And that was after I got your old boss in trouble. I'm real sorry about that." Amy sat back and took a sip of her Negroni.

"What are you talking about? Who? Mitsunaga?"

"Yep. Like I said, I'm sorry. I had no idea it would come back to haunt him. Didn't Fred tell you?"

"No, he didn't. How did you get the senator in trouble?"

"Well, I can't say much about that either. You know, it's all secret." She leaned close to Paula again. "But it was something about a spy in LA which led to the bribery scandal."

"Holy moley, are you the one who found that guy?"

"Yep. First time I nearly got myself court-martialed. But I really didn't do anything wrong. Still, people got upset. Not like the last time with Fred. That was pretty much my fault. I seem to keep finding myself on the hot seat. But, heck. That's why I'm back in Hawaii, and for that I'm not complaining. I love it here." She took another sip and signaled for the cocktail waitress. "We need to get you a drink. It's happy hour after all. Do you drink that Maker's Mark stuff like Fred? He had me try it one night. I think it nearly killed me."

Paula grimaced, sharing Amy's assessment of the popular Kentucky bourbon. She ordered a glass of red wine. "So, Amy, Fred said you met but said he couldn't really get into the details even though I had all the tickets. He said someone classified the event as 'need to know.' Called it secret decoder ring." She chuckled. "Fred."

Amy nodded.

"He's a great guy. Did you get to know him well?" Paula detected another flinch from Amy followed by the hint of a faraway smile.

"Yeah, I guess so. I mean, Mister Fred, uh, Mr. Hendricks and I spent a couple days together as we, um, how can I say this, as we worked through the issue." Amy looked down at her drink, smiling.

"Wait a minute, you two weren't . . . ?"

Amy didn't look up, but her smile grew.

"He's old enough to be your grandfather!"

"He might be old, Paula, but like I said, he saved my life on more than one occasion. And, you know, he's in really good shape for someone his age."

"Holy moley! Fred Hendricks! That old dog," Paula said, shaking her head and smirking.

"So, why are you back in Hawaii? Fred said you'd just returned to the Appropriations Committee."

Paula's wine arrived and she took a sip. It was barely drinkable. Typical for a bar, especially one that catered to a beer-and-cocktail happy hour crowd. "Yeah, well, we lost the Senate and our chairman had to resign for health reasons. And, well, it didn't really work out for my family anyway. So, I quit before they would've let me go, and we returned to Hawaii. I'm an instructor at the Asia Pacific Center. That's what I was doing before going back to DC." She shrugged. "And I understand you work in Wahiawa. Right?"

"Yup. And that's about all I can say about it." Amy winked again.

An older man wearing a bright aloha shirt and shorts with flip-flops was sitting at the bar. He had shoulder-length gray hair and was sprouting a beard. He gesticulated wildly with one hand and shouted at the bartender, "It was an SR-71, dude. Can you believe that?"

Paula looked at Amy, who had her back to the bar. "Did I just hear that guy say something about an SR-71?"

Amy nodded. "I think so. Why?"

Paula stood up. "C'mon, Amy, I want to talk to him."

Amy shrugged and said, "Okay." She picked up her drink and followed Paula to the bar.

Paula grabbed the stool on the man's left, smiling as she sat down. Amy took the seat on his right. He turned and watched Amy pull out the barstool.

"What the heck is this? Two beautiful women just happen to sit next to the old dude? I mean, yeah, double your pleasure, double your fun, but c'mon. I'm not that stupid. What's going on? Someone put you up to this?" His head turned back and forth between them several times. Then he looked at the bartender, who shrugged.

Paula grinned. "I'm sorry for eavesdropping. My name's Paula and that's Amy. But did I hear you say something about an SR-71?"

"I might have. I'm Boz." He glanced around and Amy waved. He turned back to look at Paula. "So? What's it to you?"

Paula squinted at him. "Would this have something to do with, um, a recent flight?"

"What if it did?"

"Well, let's just say that, um, well, first of all, it's a well-known fact that all the SR-71s are in museums but for maybe one exception." Paula scrunched up her nose and leaned a little closer. "You wouldn't know something about that, would you?"

"And what if I did?" He tossed back his drink.

"Maybe something about, um, let's say Kazakhstan and an Israeli."

The old guy did a double-take. He put his glass on the counter and turned on his stool to face Paula. "Russia and an American. But I can't say too much about that."

"American? What? No, that can't be right. He was Israeli."

"Well, yeah, he was an Israeli citizen, but he was an American named Jake. Told me his life story. He was born in upstate New York and his parents emigrated to Israel when he was about five to live on a kibbutz. They got killed by the PLO and he was taken in by an Israeli army officer, although by the way he talked about the guy, I'm convinced he was Mossad. You know, Israeli intelligence." He lifted his glass to get the last drop. "But I can't say much about it." He grinned at Paula.

"So, this *is* about the virus." Paula smiled. "Well, I'll be darned."

"Wait, did you say 'virus'?" Amy leaned forward so she could see around Boz and piped up, "Is this the North Korean thing?"

Boz spun around to Amy. "Now, how would you know about that?" He was nearly shouting.

Amy winked. "Well, what did you say? Oh yeah, 'I can't say much about it.'" She smiled.

Paula laughed. "Yeah, there's a lot of that going around."

Boz signaled the bartender. "I'll have another. You ladies want to try one of these?" He held up his empty glass. "It's Maker's Mark."

Amy and Paula both screamed "No!" and looked at each other, laughing.

Boz's head spun from one to the other.

II

Pat Sistrunk stepped out of his pickup truck in the strip mall parking lot in Wheeling, West Virginia. He stretched his back and flexed his knees a couple times. A few snowflakes landed on his head, so he grabbed his parka from the passenger's seat and slipped it on.

Inside Mike & Ike's Hardware, he found the gray-haired Ike stooped over behind the counter. "Hey, Ike. Where's Mike?"

"Well, well, well, if it ain't Senator Pat. You here for another freebie, Mr. Bigwig?"

From the back room Mike called out, "Who's there, Ike?"

"It's the Washington bigwig. Back for another handout."

Pat raised his hands, palms up, and shook his head. "Nope. Not this time. I still need the supplies I almost ordered back in August, but I'm not asking for a freebie. It's not for the church."

Mike popped out of the storeroom. "What time did you say dinner was, Ike? Hey, Pat. What about the church? You're not doing this work for St. Mike's?"

Pat nodded, then shook his head again. "Yeah, I was. But plans have changed. I decided to move into the house myself."

"What?" Mike questioned. "Move here? What about DC? Your job?"

"Well, gentlemen," Pat stood a little straighter and puffed out his chest. "I'm officially retired. My boss stepped down and the committee retired me."

"Hah." Ike cupped his ear. "Was that 'retired' or 'fired'? My hearing's not so good these days." He had a toothy grin. He turned toward his partner. "And dinner, Mike, is at five thirty. But don't you be late. Betty Ann won't tolerate your being late for Saturday dinner." Ike looked back at Pat.

Pat nodded again. "Yeah, Ike, I guess a little bit of both. I worked for the chairman, Senator Harry Lackland. He had a stroke and had to resign and then passed away last month. May he rest in peace. Anyway, the new chairman didn't want to keep me on. So, yeah, in a way, I was fired, but that's what happens on the Hill. And, since I've been working there so long, I qualify for retirement. So, yeah, like I said, both."

"I'll be damned. Sorry to hear about your boss, but congratulations are in order for you, I guess." Mike walked over to Pat and stuck out his hand.

Pat shook it. "Thanks. Anyways, I sold my house in Virginia, so I've got to get this one finished. No reason for me to hang around DC anymore, too many memories. I figured I'd give Wheeling Island a try."

"You're on the island, huh?" Ike spoke up with a hint of excitement.

"That's right."

"Well, then, we're neighbors." He smiled again.

"Oh yeah? You live there?" Pat asked, a touch of enthusiasm in his own voice.

"That's right. You think I could afford Woodsdale or Edgwood or the other rich-people neighborhoods?" Ike wrinkled his nose as if an off odor filled the air and slowly shook his head. "The island's fine for people like me."

"That's great," Pat responded.

Ike held up his scratch pad. "So, what you want to order?"

"Yeah, okay." Pat pulled a list from a pocket in his parka. "I need paint, maybe white, something not top-of-the-line, but good. And enough drywall for an eleven- by twelve-foot room."

Ike wrote it down and calculated the amount. "That'll be $500."

"What?" Mike squawked. "How's that possible? It's got to be at least $550 for all that."

Ike looked at his partner, lifted his chin, and said. "I'm giving Pat the neighbor discount, Mike. You got a problem with that?"

Mike stood there with his mouth open. He looked back and forth between Ike and Pat. "Well, I'll be damned."

Ike turned to Pat. "We need twenty percent down today—one

hundred dollars—and the balance on Monday, when you can pick up the supplies. Is that cash or charge?"

Pat pulled out his wallet and laid two fifties on the counter. "My ATM machine only gives out fifties. That's all the cash I got. You guys tell me where there's an ATM around here? I need to get some more cash for dinner."

"Why don't you join Mike and me for dinner?" Ike asked.

"Really?" Pat was shocked. "It's been a long time since I had a home-cooked meal. You sure your wife is okay with something like that?"

"Oh yeah, Betty Ann loves to have a houseful. As long as you're on time, your hands ain't dirty, and you got on a clean shirt."

The look of surprise remained on Mike's face.

"What are you looking at me for, you old fool?" Ike snapped. "We's neighbors," he said, throwing a hand at Pat across the counter and glaring at his partner.

Pat thanked them both, smiling into the faux fur of his collar.

As he exited the store, the little bell on the door signaled his departure.

Pat noted the tinkling. *What's that they say about a bell ringing? Oh yeah, another angel got its wings. Attaboy, Harry.*

TO THE READER

The 101st Senator is a work of fiction. The events and characters portrayed are from the author's imagination or used fictitiously. By my research, I believe the first time a Senate staff member was referred to as "the hundred and first senator" was in the late 1950s when a key member of Lyndon Johnson's staff earned himself the moniker by wielding influence far beyond his official staff position. When I joined the staff in the early 1980s, I was told that the staff director of the Senate Appropriations Committee was frequently referred to as the hundred and first senator because of the importance of his position. However, I only found one reference in the press to a former staff director being so labeled, in a 2008 *Politico* article.

The genesis of this book is a vignette, perhaps apocryphal, shared with me by another longtime Senate staffer. In the 1960s, his boss, then a freshman senator from the Deep South seeking a position on a specific committee, was granted a meeting with the committee chairman. He found the elderly chairman and his wife seated on a couch in the chairman's office. The senior senator said nothing and appeared incapacitated while his wife did all the talking. The junior senator stormed out of the meeting after listening to the wife repeatedly explain what the senior senator was supposedly thinking, shouting, "Well, if the senator is *thinking*, you sure can't tell!"

Again, I am grateful to family, friends, and Emerald Editorial Services for bearing with me as I worked my way through another novel. I'm particularly in the debt of a few former air force officers from the "SR community" who helped me portray what the SR-71 might be capable of were it still flying today. I alone am responsible for all errors.

ALSO BY C J HOUY

VIGILANTE POLITICS (2017). When a distinguished senator is exposed taking campaign money from the Chinese military, Paula Means, a brilliant and beautiful Senate staffer, gets caught in the crossfire. Sidelined by the scandal, she watches conniving politicians vie for the presidency and hurl the world toward nuclear Armageddon. It's up to Paula, along with military and civilian leaders, to stop the madness.

SENATE INTELLIGENCE (2019). Melissa O'Brien knows everything about classified satellites and space technology but little of life and love. Now she's entering the byzantine world of arcane rules and practices at the Senate Intelligence Committee, where friend and foe, success and failure can be mirror images. But the story opens in Paris where a young man is asked, "What happened to the girl?"

SHOOT THE STAFF (2020). Fred Hendricks, with a creaky back and chronic heartburn, is retiring from the United States Senate staff after forty years. But first, in a new assignment as the lead staffer for the Senate Appropriations Subcommittee on Defense, he has to shepherd one last appropriations bill to enactment. His hopes for a smooth process are dashed when a whistleblower whispers about an NSA scheme to rig elections. Coupled with an upstart junior senator who challenges the bipartisan traditions of the Appropriations Committee, her short-tempered senior colleague who has a strained party history, and an unchained president seeking to safeguard his reelection and you get to *Shoot the Staff*.

Printed in the USA
CPSIA information can be obtained
at www.ICGtesting.com
LVHW040904150923
758219LV00002B/157